Battling for the Heavens

Grug Smash Book 3

Sean McKenzie

CONTENTS

CHAPTER 1

A PLAN GONE WRONG

The plan had been perfect; it had seemed perfect, Grug amended mentally. Now here he sat. The rain ran in rivulets through the tiny, barred window to the outside, while the damp earth outside the dungeon's walls leeched moisture through the mortar between the rough-hewn stone blocks. Grug's shackles bore a gritty, red skin of rust that had rubbed away on the inside from his straining to test their durability. Sadly, it seemed as likely that the chain would somehow break free of the stone as that the chain itself would break; neither seemed likely, but Grug found himself yearning to hear the roll of dice, to give him at least a glimmering hope of success.

Grinding his teeth, Grug tried to force his brain to come up with an idea. His shoulders bunched, his neck and arms swelled up, and each muscle of his chest and abdomen appeared chiseled from living marble. None of it helped Grug flex what he thought must be his brain muscles, and no plan for escape unfolded in his mind.

Grug leaned his head back against the damp wall with a sigh. He didn't need the dice to tell him he had failed: failed to retrieve the amulet; failed to defeat the sorcerer; perhaps failed to save the world. The truth of that was lodged in his very bones. Not for the first time, Grug wondered if his friends had made it out of the palace. Misery welled up inside of him, doubling him over, and nausea wracked him. It was his fault, all his fault, if they hadn't made it out. Gods above, Grug hated being stupid.

Hours passed. Grug oscillated between depression, self-loathing, and brief flickers of hope, during which he would rally long enough to strain against his bonds and curse the growing raw spots on his wrists. Always, though, his eye would return to the small window, watching as the shadows of the rain clouds dispersed, and the sun began to shine— though not so much as a stray beam found its way past the buildings outside and into the cell. The sunlight was for others, not for Grug; for Grug, there was only the reflection of warmth and brightness that the light held.

*   *   *

It's not that it's impossible," Samuel said, moving the candleholder off the sketched map of the palace and out of the way. "It's just going to be much more difficult than you're making it out to be."

"Why?" Oma Matawa, the stout, olive faced head of the smuggling faction demanded. "We've smuggled goods out of those sewers before."

Samuel exchanged a glance with Olan Delana, the major heist faction leader. "How large are the goods you've passed through there, Oma?" Olan asked. "Anything the size of, say, our barbarian friend's shoulders, over there?" He nodded to Grug, who was sitting quietly in the corner of Samuel's thieves guild office, near the fire. The pallet Grug had occupied while healing had been moved out of the room, and replaced with a number of chairs, most of which now held the other members of Grug's party: Bhalon Lightbringer, a dwarven cleric; Haeronor Spelltwister, an elven mage; Triwathon Arrowborn, an elven ranger; and Giselle Rana'Ghal, an orcish warrior.

Olan sighed, leaning more heavily on the large, wooden table they had moved into the center of the room to spread maps upon. "Giselle's shoulders wouldn't fit either; we'd have to strip the two of them and coat them in grease to have any hope of getting them through the sewer access."

"If that's a proposition, it's a poor one," Giselle said. "I'd avoid leading with an invitation to the sewers, especially."

Olan laughed, clearly charmed by the beautiful orcess, as nearly everyone who met her seemed to be. "I wouldn't dream of offending you, my lady. I do think it's best we avoid the sewers altogether."

"There have been some small goods moved over the wall," Oma said slowly. "This large a group, though, would be a challenge. Is there any chance we could buy the postern gate guard?"

Samuel frowned thoughtfully from across the table. "It's not impossible, but with the sorcerer's ability to take over bodies, how could we be sure who is and who isn't compromised? Worse, there's bound to be at least two guards at the gate, and another pair to switch shifts with them close by. Four times the men is four times the risk."

Oma nodded slowly. "Well, unless we find a way for all of you to learn how to fly, or we want to try an offensive on the main gate, scaling the wall may be the only option left to us. You're proficient enough, guild master, but how much experience does the rest of your group have with climbing?"

Samuel gestured to Grug. "I've seen Grug climb; he'll do fine. I expect the elves will do fine as well." Haeronor and Triwathon nodded. "Bhalon? Giselle?"

Bhalon muttered into his beard.

Samuel looked perplexed. Giselle met his eyes and shrugged. "What was that, Bhalon?" Samuel asked.

The dwarf glared. "I do no' like heights," he said at last. "And I'm no' exactly built for climbin'." He blushed as dark a red as his beard.

"I do well enough with trees," Giselle said quickly, giving Bhalon a chance to recover from his obvious embarrassment, "but I'm not so practiced at walls—especially if I'm armoured."

"You wouldn't be," Samuel said, "at least, not in plate mail. It would be too bulky—and far too loud. The goal here is to be neither seen, nor heard, so we'll be in blackened leather. I can offer clawed gloves to help with the climb, as well, but they really only help if you're already a reasonably practiced climber. Bhalon, it may be better if you stayed behind. We're likely to be going over roofs, as well as walls. Having someone who's…who doesn't like heights, will be difficult."

Bhalon bristled defensively. "I'll no' be left behind like a child!" he snapped. "And ye've no other protection against the sorcerer's blood magic. Ye'd be fools to go in without me!"

"You're absolutely right," Samuel said placatingly. "We would stand little chance against the sorcerer's blood magic without you. But again, our aim here is to avoid detection—not to fight. The longer we take getting over the wall, and the more noise we make doing it, the more likely we are to attract the attention of sentries, above and below. A protracted fight of any kind would likely mean forfeiting any hope of infiltration."

Grug had been working on something to say, but Samuel could see him sit back in his chair, trying to work out Samuel's words and feeling driven out of the conversation. "Sorry, Grug," Samuel said, "did you have something you wanted to add?"

Grug looked up in surprise, and struggled to put his words together. "Need more help. Bhalon-go-dwarves," he blurted.

The group exchanged confused looks, except for Giselle, who studied Grug thoughtfully. "That's actually a very good idea, Grug," she said.

Grug's uncertain face broke into a broad smile at being understood.

"Care to enlighten the rest of us?" Triwathon asked.

"If you actually listened to Grug, you wouldn't need me to," Giselle chided. "Grug was pointing out that we need more help. We have the thieves guilds, potentially, and perhaps the gnomes, as well. If Bhalon could convince the dwarves to join us…"

"Ye'll not send me off on some fool's errand," Bhalon objected.

"She may have a point, Bhalon," Samuel mused. "The dwarf clans should know what's going on, one way or the other. If you have any connections in the various clans, it would certainly be worth the effort to try convincing them to join our cause."

Bhalon grunted sourly. "And why does it have to be done right now, when yer makin' yer way through the castle to get the amulet?"

"It doesn't," Samuel said sharply. "What it does do is remove a situation where you will not only imperil your own life, but the rest of ours, as well. Is that enough of a reason?"

Bhalon blushed a fiery red, turned abruptly, and left the room. The door slamming behind him was enough to knock a picture off of the wall behind Oma, and onto the floor.

After a moment of uncomfortable silence, Grug asked softly: "why Samuel be so mean to Bhalon?"

Samuel looked at Grug with tired, sad eyes. "Because it's the only way he'll listen to me, my friend. I'll not risk his life, and ours, on his pride."

"It's not the first time Bhalon's pride has been hurt," Haeronor said. "It will heal. You did well, guild master."

Giselle nodded in agreement. "We really should send an envoy to the dwarfs, anyway. This is as good an opportunity as any. Sending someone to the barbarians in Narran may be useful, too." Her mouth twisted in distaste. "I will send a letter to my…fellow orcs, as well. If they're already mobilizing, we may be able to guide where they go, and what front they threaten."

Samuel nodded thoughtfully. "You're right; it's past time that we let them know what's going on. But I think it would be better for you to speak with your father face to face."

Giselle shot Samuel a furious glare before glancing quickly over at Grug to see if he had caught the meaning of Samuel's words.

"It's past time, Giselle," Samuel said. "It's not fair to leave Grug the only one in our group who doesn't know."

Grug looked at Giselle in confusion. "What Grug not know?"

Giselle glared at Samuel again before she turned to the barbarian. "Grug, my full name is Giselle Rana'Ghal. My father is B'Haratruk Ghal, the Nalrag of Southern Haeraxa.

Grug stared blankly at her.

"Nalrag is like a warchief…or a king."

Grug nodded as he thought through her words. "So Giselle is…princess?"

"Yes."

"Okay," Grug said simply.

Giselle was taken aback. "Doesn't that bother you, at all?"

Grug appeared to think very hard for a moment, his face contorted as though he was trying to lift a load too heavy for him. Finally, his smile returned. "No," he said.

"Oh." Giselle was momentarily speechless. "Well, good. Just don't expect me to show up in a pink ball gown or anything like that."

Grug laughed. "Funny picture."

Giselle grinned, her prominent canine teeth hanging from her mouth. "I suppose it is, isn't it? Now, if I'm to be traveling back to meet with my father, we best finish planning how you're going to get in and out of the castle. You men would probably plan your way right into the dungeon without me," she said glibly. "Now, Olan—"

*   *   *

As the shadows deepened, and the day came to a close, Grug could hear the snapping of locks and bolts down the long corridor that led to his cell. Light flickered beyond the small grate in the heavy, iron-banded cell door, as a torch bobbed lazily down the corridor toward Grug's cell. After a few moments, the torch bearer halted, and there was more metallic grating and a heavy thunk as the lock on his door was opened. With all the grace and majesty of his position, the king strode into the small cell, careful to stay beyond Grug's shackled reach.

Grug's fists clenched, as he tried to work out a way to get a loop of his chain around the sorcerer's throat. He let his mind wander for a moment, picturing standing over the sorcerer's body, the face purple, and the lungs airless, and then forced himself back to the present situation.

The sorcerer stared down at Grug. "That will be all," he said to the jailer.

"But yer Majesty, the prisoner is dangerous! Surely—"

The sorcerer quelled the man's words with a glance, and the jailer put the torch into a socket just inside the cell door before backing out of the room, head bowed. Grug listened to the jailer's footsteps retreat down the dark corridor, while forcing himself to stay motionless and meet the sorcerer's gaze. After what seemed an eternity, he heard the jailer unlock the jail door again and let himself out.

Waves of malevolence seared at Grug's soul, but the proud barbarian would not bend his neck. At last, the sorcerer broke the silence. "You complete and utter imbecile. Did you imagine, for even a moment, that you could outsmart me? You, and that ridiculous band of fools? I am the most powerful sorcerer in the world!

Grug ignored the specks of spittle that struck his face, staring at the sorcerer with eyes full of hatred.

"I will catch your friends, Grug, all of them. But what shall we do with you in the meantime?"

Grug felt a momentary elation when he realized that the sorcerer's words meant that his friends had escaped. "You kill Grug," he ventured, as last.

The sorcerer's slow smile promised endless horrors, not a quick death. "Perhaps eventually, barbarian. But not yet. First, I will break your spirit, as I have broken your mind by taking the amulet away from you. You will crawl for me; you will beg to do my bidding, to please me." He waved a hand, and Grug felt himself frozen in place. The sorcerer drew a small, silver dagger from his belt and sliced slowly across Grug's cheek. Unhurriedly, he wiped the blade on the barbarian's hair and re-sheathed it, next pulling out a small, flat stone from his belt pouch. Grug winced as the sorcerer dragged the stone across the fresh cut, scraping the exposed inner tissues and coating the rock in blood.

The sorcerer leaned close, his face as close to Grug's as a lover's, his eyes riveted on the barbarian's own. "And now your soul is mine."

The sorcerer stood, taking the torch from its socket, and walked out of the room. Grug heard the locks snap shut again, as the sorcerer left him in a darkness deeper than any he had ever known. If the plan had seemed so perfect, why was he hanging here now?

CHAPTER 2

MARRED PERFECTION

In the deepest shadows, at the darkest hour of night, five figures stood, gazing up at the palace walls. One figure, far shorter than the rest, crept next to the wall itself, gently stroking the stone and whispering softly for a moment before melting back into the shadows and rejoining its companions.

"Is there," Shalevelkin said. "Amulet is in tower."

"You're certain?" Haeronor whispered.

The gnomish stonesinger nodded, a movement lost in the darkness to all but Haeronor's keen, elven eyes. "The stone knows."

"Right, then," Olan said. "Let's get moving." He slipped away across the cobbled street and into the shadows of the castle wall.

Samuel bowed to the stocky stonesinger. "Thank you, Gnarrinshang."

The gnome deeply in acknowledgement and disappeared into the darkness of the alleyway. Samuel slipped silently into the night and rejoined his companions, where Olan was already handing around clawed climbing gloves to all but Haeronor, who had disdainfully refused the offer while they were readying the gear for their heist. As he slipped on his own pair of gloves on, Samuel searched the rooftops for any sight of Triwathon, but the ranger had left not so much as a hint of where he might be—his form blended seamlessly into the shadows of whichever roof he occupied.

Clearly, Haeronor didn't have the same difficulty. "Ten count," he whispered, interpreting Triwathon's signal. "Get ready."

They lined up against the wall, their clawed gloves scraping quietly against the stone, but sounding inordinately loud in the silence of the night. At Haeronor's command, they began to climb. Samuel and Olan moved like the professionals they were, swiftly pulling themselves from handhold to handhold with careful grace. Haeronor seemed to flow up the wall, to Grug's eye, barely pausing between handholds and moving far faster than Grug could ever hope to do. To be completely fair though, Grug thought, he was carrying three bags strapped to his back, while Haeronor carried only himself.

"Hurry," the elf hissed back to Grug," or we're going to have to find ourselves another barbarian."

Grug glared at the mage, knowing that the elf's keen eyes would pick it up in the darkness. A small chuckle floated back.

They climbed the rest of the way to what seemed like mid-way to the top in silence and clung like black burrs to the stone. The soft jingling of mail floated down from the top of the wall, as the sentries crossed paths almost directly above their heads. Grug imagined Triwathon crouched on a nearby roof, arrow already on the string of his bow and ready to fire if either sentry happened to glance downward and spot them. Fortunately, neither guard appeared to be particularly good at his job; they passed uneventfully, looking more at each other's shiny armour than at the darkness beyond their torches. After a patient ten-count, Haeronor led them up the remaining wall and over the battlement.

The top of the wall was about ten feet wide and made entirely of limestone, with short spans leading in from the wall itself to small towers that provided both stone stairwells down to the courtyard, and small guardhouses, where those on duty could warm themselves on colder nights. Grug had pulled himself over the top of the ramparts and was reaching back down to pull Olan over when a third sentry suddenly stepped out from the guardhouse. A young man, the soft peach fuzz of his first beard barely turned to coarser whiskers, and the self-importance of his new position drawn about him like a cloak, he chose to confront the group directly, rather than sound the alarm. Even his chainmail seemed to jingle pompously as he stormed up to Grug. "And what is the meaning of this?" he demanded. "You are trespassing on the King's own property!"

Grug gaped at him, even as he swung Olan over the top of the battlement.

"You will submit yourselves for judgement, and accompany me forthwith—"

Grug's fist, still covered with a tough leather climbing gauntlet, caught the guard's chin with a crisp straight right. Arrogantly sure and ironically unguarded, the guard flew back as though kicked by a horse and skidded a full five paces along the top of the wall. Almost before he came to a halt, Grug was striding toward him. The barbarian grabbed the front of the guardsman's tunic, lifting him so that only his feet dragged on the ground, and carried him swiftly back to the guardhouse from whence he had emerged. He slung the unconscious form into the squat, stone room with a muffled crash, before turning back to join Olan, Samuel, and Haeronor, who were already trotting quietly down the stone steps and into the courtyard.

This late, only one torch in three was kept burning, leaving ample shadows for even Grug to hide in. Dirt and gravel crunched softly beneath the party's boots as they made their way back between a small cache of bales and barrels, stored within a nook in the inner wall, and a goat pen. They crouched, concealed for the moment, and waited for the signal.

"Get off, you filthy beast," Olan hissed. Grug glanced over at the stocky major heist leader and nearly let out a laugh. A small brown and white goat had pushed its head through the rails of its pen and was nuzzling Olan, pushing its head into his side and looking for attention. Olan pushed it away, and the goat bleated mournfully at him, trying to work its way back under his arm, but Samuel pulled a handful of hay from one of the bales stacked in the cache, throwing it down near the animal. The goat looked torn for a moment, unsure of whether to choose free food, or the potential for further attentions from Olan, but it ultimately turned its attentions to the sure bet of the hay.

Yells sounded from the walls, and Samuel slid quietly up near the front of the cache for a moment. He returned moments later. "It looks like our distraction is in place. The guards all seem to be over on the east wall, watching the fires."

Olan nodded, a tight smile on his face. "Right. Let's get moving, then."

They moved almost silently through the shadow of the wall, listening to the now quite audible crackling of thatch coming from the merchant's stalls on the other side of the wall. Grug felt a momentary pang of conscience at the need to burn the stalls, but Samuel had carefully explained that the stalls were the best choice for a distraction, as it was unlikely that anyone would be injured, even if some lost their possessions. It still seemed unfair and mean, Grug thought.

Within moments, they had slipped through the servants' door and into the corridors. The halls were quiet in the early hours, as the thieves had hoped; even those on cleaning and polishing detail had long since finished their work and sought their beds, and it was still too early for the bakers to begin on the morning's bread. The party moved carefully in the silence, moving between the decorative nooks that lined the hall at ten-pace intervals. At each nook, they paused, listening for any sound of approaching footsteps, but there was only a crypt-like silence.

The party soon reached a wide stone staircase, spiraling up into the darkness off the upper floors. Olan stepped past Samuel to take the lead, his shoulder pressed close to the inner wall of the stair, and his long knife held naked in his left hand. The thief had been adamant during planning that he lead, being the only left-handed one in the group. Armed with a shorter blade, Olan would be able to strike swiftly at anyone coming down the stair, silencing them before they could cry out. While Grug agreed with the logic, after it was painstakingly explained to him, he was clearly uncomfortable with letting Olan lead. He carried himself well, but he was so…well…small. So was his weapon, when compared to Grug's sword.

Tendrils of light danced over the darkened stone only moments before the sound of footsteps warned them of someone approaching. The party flattened themselves against the inner wall of the stair as the steps grew closer, hardly daring to breath. Olan seemed to tense like a coiled spring, his left arm pulling his blade back past his hip, while his right hand opened and his arm extended, preparing to grab hold of the unlucky late roamer.

The man emerged, holding a smoking torch. Grug cursed silently when he saw the gleam of a breastplate; it would have to be a fully-armoured king's guard on his nightly rounds. Olan didn't hesitate for a moment. The thief's heel hooked behind the other man's even as his hand closed over the knight's mouth and forced him back onto the stairs with a muffled clank—the heavy metal backplate quieted by the flesh above it. Before the guard could move his hand toward a weapon, Olan had found the space between the breast and back plates, sliding his knife up beneath the ribs, expertly angled toward the man's heart. The guard's body tensed for a moment, and fell still.

Olan slid his blade back out and wiped it on the sleeve of the guard's tunic before standing again. Grug thought he looked taller, somehow. "There's nowhere to hide the body without making more noise moving it," Olan whispered. "We need to hurry, and hope the next guard shift is running late."

Samuel nodded and motioned Olan to lead on. They took the stairs at a trot, doing their best to balance their desire for silence with their need for speed. Grug peered curiously toward each arrow slit they passed, watching the small blur of torches in the courtyard and on the wall fall lower in his view until they were gradually swallowed by the darkness of the night.

They stopped at the upper landing of the stairs, where a massive, iron-strapped wooden door barred their entry. There was no guard in sight—which meant that one or more awaited them within, or that the one they had met on the way up was, in fact, awaiting his replacement for a shift change. Olan pulled a set of lock picks from his sleeve. "Ready yourselves; we need to be quick," he whispered.

Haeronor touched Olan's shoulder, motioning him back, and pulled a jade tree, just slightly larger than his palm, out from his belt pouch. He held it for a moment, muttering under his breath, and the tree began to glow softly, bathing the landing in green. For a moment, Grug could smell the fresh scent of pine needles, mixed with the spicier smell of decaying leaves. Haeronor pressed the tree gently against the door lock, and it turned an angry red that left Grug's mouth tasting of copper. The two colours warred for a moment in the talisman, a flickering dance of attack and retreat, before the green finally overtook and consumed the angry taint of the sorcerer's spell. Haeronor stepped back and nodded to Olan.

Nodding his thanks to the elven mage, Olan pulled a pick and a tensioner from his lockpick set. Kneeling down, he slid them into the lock, his eyes closed as he felt for the pins. After a few moments, the thief twisted the tensioner, gently swinging the door open just enough to peer into the dark room within. After a moment, the thief carefully levered the door open enough to slip through, listening carefully for any creak or groan from the hinge. Haeronor took the thief's place at the door, his long elven fingers updating the rest of the party on Olan's progress.

Olan made his way through the dark room, his eyes slowly adjusting to faint rays of moonlight filtering through a light curtain to the balcony and a pair of windows set high in the curving walls, near the top of the vaulted ceiling. The room was silent but for a soft snore coming from the oversized, four-posted bed, with heavy satin drapes, behind which the sorcerer slept. Olan flowed from shadow to shadow with every ounce of skill he possesses, moving like a trail of drifting smoke more than a man. His eyes scanned the room endlessly for signs of traps, or of the amulet, though his gut told him that it would be as near to the sorcerer as was practical.

Olan was nearly at the foot of the bed when he finally made out the shape of the amulet, laid on the chest of the most grotesque mannequin he had ever seen, its face a distorted mockery of a man's, the granite "flesh" melted like candle wax, with eyes like endless black pits. Olan glided silently to the mannequin, one eye on the bed curtains. Carefully placing his feet to avoid a pair of bizarrely fluffy slippers, Olan reached toward the mannequin's neck, gently lifting the links of chain from the granite shoulders, and muffling the clinking with his hands.

The mannequin blinked.

Olan's professional demeanour survived intact, right up until the mannequin grabbed onto his arms and opened its maw to expose finger-long fangs and a fiery glow like the bowels of hell. Then he screamed like a 12-year old girl. Behind the curtains, a shadowy figure jerked awake just in time for the first of Haeronor's fireballs to strike the bed, as the rest of the party charged into the room. The flames raced around a shield spell, an invisible orb that quickly leeched away the heat and light of the fire. Olan was thrown back through the charring tongues toward the group, sliding in an unconscious heap at Samuel's feet.

With Olan out of the line of fire, Haeronor erupted like a box of fireworks thrown on bonfire. Previously-prepared spells that the mage had painstakingly set for days before the heist triggered one after another, some catching and absorbing the spells flying from the other side of the bed, while others rained fire, lighting and pure energy down on the demonic mannequin and its master.

Grug had raised his axe to charge in when Samuel's hand pulled him up short. The thief wasted no time towing his barbarian friend toward the balcony. "The ropes, Grug!" Samuel bellowed above the sound of miniature explosions. "We have to get the hell out of here!" Grug stared blankly for a moment before he remembered the heavy ropes coiled in his bag. He pushed through the balcony curtain at a jog, already slinging the bag from his back. Behind him, the air continued to crackle and roar, as Haeronor fought to keep the sorcerer from mounting an effective offense. Samuel dashed back through the curtain while Grug tied the rope onto a pair of thick, stone balustrades, returning a moment later dragging Olan, who appeared to have regained consciousness, but could not yet support his own weight.

Grug left Samuel to the task of getting Olan down the rope and ran back through the curtain. Without a word, he dashed up beside Haeronor, grabbed the mage around the waist and spun, bodily throwing him toward the balcony and trusting the elf's inborn grace to help him land on his feet, rather than his face. The barbarian managed one bounding stride toward his companions before something that felt roughly the size and weight of a stone horse plowed into his back, knocking him to the ground and driving the air from his lungs.

"Leave him to me," Grug heard the sorcerer roar. "Get the others!" As the weight on his back shifted, Grug rolled with it, catching the demon around the legs and bringing it back down to its knees. His axe long since lost in the confusion, Grug pulled his dagger desperately from his belt sheathe and slammed in into the demon's back. For all his strength, no more than half of the blade made it past the demon's rocky skin, but it was enough to make the fiend buck and shriek, spattering Grug with glowing blood that seared its way into the flesh of his hands. Fighting against the pain, Grug strained, pulling the dagger back out and raising it to strike again, but magical bonds encircled his arms, wrenching him back and throwing him to the floor. Grug's last sight before he lost consciousness was a pair of pink, fluffy slippers. Idly, he wondered if the sorcerer had chosen them himself, or if they were the only colour available.

CHAPTER 3

HOMECOMING

Bhalon stopped walking when he was a single pace onto dwarven lands, staring down a broad path to the iron-bound gate of the Dragonstooth Kinsfolk's dwarvenhome. His body hummed with a feeling of power and solidness that told him he had arrived on the lands of his people, and was welcome.

An old dwarven proverb spoke of it being impossible to knock a dwarf from his feet in his own home, and it wasn't far from the truth; every one of the Dragonstooth Kinsfolk would feel the same unshakeable strength and fortitude in their home. This was in no small part why dwarves so infrequently warred with one another—to siege a fortress built into a mountain was foolish; to siege one where every enemy was stronger solely by virtue of their kinship was suicide. Much more frequent were revolutions, but even those were rare, as the Knitting Circle had a long memory and a volatile temper.

Bhalon resumed walking, but had taken no more than two steps when a high voice rang out: "Hold! State your kin and your business here." It took Bhalon a moment to find the speaker; he finally picked out a small, rectangular hole chiselled through a rock wall that must have been much slimmer than it appeared from the front.

"My name is Bhalon Lightbringer, cleric o' the High Lord, and dwarf of the Dragonstooth Kinsfolk. Who stands guard for the teeth o' the dragon?"

An unsurprisingly stocky figure tramped out from behind the boulder, fully armoured and with a heavy crossbow in hand. The warrior motioned Bhalon forward, the bolt still trained on the cleric's heart. Bhalon tried, unsuccessfully, to guess who the warrior might be, but nothing seemed to penetrate the fog in his brain that surrounded his past. While random facts seemed to swirl everywhere in his mind, he couldn't remember a single person he had known growing up. The guard's heavy plate, bare of any family sigil, other than the Dragonstooth crest, made it difficult to judge even if the guard was male or female. It occurred to Bhalon that perhaps certain adaptations could be made to female armour to make the wearer's sex more obvious, rather than accommodating such things in the layers of padding beneath the breastplate, but he couldn't think of a particularly good reason to do so. Extra angles would just make it more likely that a sword or axe would catch, rather than sliding off. In any event, the questions was soon rendered moot when the warrior raised her visor.

"So it is you," she said. "Welcome home."

Clearly the speaker knew him, but try as he might, he couldn't dredge up so much as a hint in his memory. "You too," he said awkwardly.

The woman raised one eyebrow far enough that it retreated beneath her upraised visor. "Well, you certainly haven't become any smoother since you left. You always were hopeless with anything female, weren't you—though I didn't think I counted that way, to you. I remember you with Susie Landstooth, though; for all your mooning over here and wistful staring, you threw up on her shoes the first time you tried to really talk to her. Mind you," the dwarfess said thoughtfully, "I guess that was an improvement overall. You mostly just pulled her hair and threw snowballs at her before that."

Bhalon stood, nonplussed. "Aye. Well, I must meet with the Knittin' Circle immediately. If ya could take me ta them…"

The woman tore her helmet off, staring at him incredulously. Her face was broad, heavy boned, with a muscular jaw—undeniably attractive by dwarfish standards. "Bhalon, it's Anala—how do you not remember me? Have you taken a head wound?"

Bhalon seized on her suggestion desperately. "Yes, tha's exactly it. A terrible head wound. Canno' remember much of anything."

"Oh." She seemed hurt, and Bhalon wished he could think of something comforting to say. "Well," she said at last, perhaps you've forgotten how the Knitting Circle works as well, then. They send for you, not the other way around. If I took you in there without them calling for you, your mother would have the flesh off both our backsides."

"My mother?" Bhalon asked.

Anala quirked a shaggy eyebrow. "Who else would head the Circle? How hard did you get hit?" She turned back toward the mountain face and whistled sharply. An armoured figure, visor lowered, and crossbow still pointed toward Bhalon, tramped out from an opening just to the left of the gates and trotted toward them. When the guard neared them, Anala called: "This is Bhalon, son of Mara. I'm going to take him in to await the call of the Circle." The other dwarf nodded, taking Anala's place behind the stone wall, as Anala led Bhalon past and down the path toward the entrance to the Dragonstooth kingdom.

The gate was simple, unadorned, and seamless. It didn't fasten or span a gap in the cliff, for there was no permanent gap in the stone; as they approached, the gate seemed to melt away, rather than open, recognizing their blood and receding into the rock around it, to grant them entrance. The two passed into a maze of passages that Bhalon couldn't begin to memorize, but Anala clearly knew intimately. Their footfalls echoed hollowly through the caverns, amplified and muddled by the rounded ceilings and their rough stone faces. Glass tubes sprouted forth from the ceiling periodically, bringing sunlight down into what would have been uninterrupted darkness.

Anala broke the silence, at last, her voice clipped and brusque. "I'll take you to your father while you await the Circle's call. I trust you'll remember him, at least."

Bhalon's stomach twisted anxiously. Try as he might, he could remember nothing of his father, his mind conjuring only an image of his own face, but craggier and older. "Where is he like ta' be?" Bhalon asked.

Anala looked at him as though he'd grown a second head. "In the kitchens, of course. Where else?" She studied him silently for a moment, and whatever she saw stopped her so suddenly that Bhalon nearly tripped over her. "You really don't remember anything, do you?"

Bhalon looked at his feet, his face burning, and slowly shook his head.

"Tharmekhûl!" Anala swore. "Nothing? Your parents?"

Bhalon struggled to meet her eyes, shame threatening to overwhelm him, and shook his head.

"That must have been quite the blow to the head. Mace?"

"Boulder," Bhalon replied.

Anala whistled. "What do you remember, then?"

Bhalon shrugged. "No' much. Facts, mostly, like I read 'em ina book. I knew how ta' get here; I know abou' the power o' being kinsfolk in our own lands; but I do no' remember people or many details abou' the clan."

Anala blew out a long breath. "Sorry, Bhalon. That's awful. Is that why you're talking so oddly, too?"

"I dunno wha' you—"

"Bhalon?" a deep voice called from the next intersection. "Is that you?"

An older dwarf emerged from the shadows and into the light of the nearest sky tube. He was unsurprisingly squat, with forearms roughly the size of Bhalon's thighs, it seemed, and a long, red beard streaked through with grey. "It is, burn me! Welcome home, son!"

Before Bhalon knew what was happening, he had been swept up in an embrace a python might have envied, with only the thickness of his dwarven ribs keeping them from breaking. At last, he was released and left drawing deep breaths, wincing as his new bruises stretched.

"Svellin," Anala said respectfully, "I was just bringing Bhalon to you. He is awaiting the call of the Knitting Circle."

Svellin surveyed Bhalon thoughtfully. "It must be awfully important for you to brave that thicket of thorns."

"T'tis," Bhalon replied. "I—"

Svellin waved his hands dismissively. "No, son; there will be time enough for that once the Knitting Circle has heard what you have to say. By the Maker, it's wonderful to have you home!" He crushed Bhalon in a hug again. "Come, son. I was just heading to the kitchens. We can talk more there."

Bhalon's heart lurched in his chest like he'd just taken a swing from an ogre's maul, and he tried not to stare at the older dwarf. His...father.

Anala gripped his shoulder with one broad, scarred hand, and gave him a sad, understanding smile. "Go, Bhalon. We can catch up later." She turned and marched back toward her post, heavy armour clanking and reflecting pinpricks of light through the corridors.

Svellin gave Bhalon a broad smile and gestured for his son to walk beside him. The two walked without speaking for a moment, Svellin in companionable silence, while Bhalon desperately tried to distract himself by tracing veins and transitions in the stone around them. Torchlight replaced the natural light of the sun tubes as the corridor led progressively deeper into the mountain's heart.

"Your mother will be pleased to see you," Svellin said at last. "It's been a long time since you've been home."

"Aye," Bhalon replied glibly. "I barely remember tha' place, it seems."

Svellin shot him a confused look. "You must have travelled far into the mountains, then, have you? You sound like the dwarven folk of old—before we even became the kinfolk."

"What d'ya mean?" Bhalon asked.

"That accent, son. Dwarves in the south haven't sounded like that since your grandfather's grandfather, when we were all still broken into named clans, instead of the five kinsfolk. The only place I've heard someone speak like you was in a mummer's show, though I've heard there are still dwarves deep in the northern mountains that have the same accent. Did you stay with them for a time?"

"No," Bhalon said. "I guess I must ha' picked it up somewhere else." He paused uncomfortably for a moment. "There's something more important we need ta worry abou', righ' now. The reason I came back—"

"No, son. I'll not hear it before the Circle does. Your mother would have my head for a wool basket. You know what the Circle is like."

"Then we must go straight to them," Bhalon said decisively. "It canno' wait."

Svellin stared at Bhalon as though he had just suggested a quick jog across an ocean and a swim in a volcano. "Are you mad, son? You'd be lucky to escape with your ears attached! The Circle summons *you* to *it*; it has been that way since we stopped warring and became kin. Did your travels unhinge your wits?" Svellin turned down a dark, narrow corridor to their left. Bhalon followed, emerging into a cozy kitchen, snuggled into the centre of the kinsfolk home.

Though hewn from the rock, the kitchen was remarkably clean. Every surface seemed to be made of well-polished granite or marble, veins and flecks of colourful silicates dancing merrily through the stone. Metal and wood, where it was used at all, fastened invisibly, seeming to grow forth from the stone with no need of screws or hinges. Strange orbs hung in sconces of silver, flooding the kitchen with a warm, bright light.

"Are those jrel?" Bhalon asked, pointing to the globes. "Hearts o' the mountain? I thought 'em rare enough ta be saved only for special rooms."

Svellen had opened a small stone door in one wall and begun digging around in it. He pulled a large, brown, ceramic bowl from a shelf and turned to look quizzically at his son. "And what room could possibly be more important than a kitchen?" He laid the bowl down carefully on the marble counter between him and his son, and pulled a cloth from overtop it to reveal a soft, brownish dough. "You haven't discovered a way to live without eating while on your adventures, have you?" Svellin's tone was serious, but his dark eyes sparkled with humour.

Bhalon, feeling flustered, shook his head and gave an embarrassed smile. He watched his father dust the stone surface of the counter with flour and scrape the dough from its container.

The kitchen soon echoed softly with the sounds of Svellin's kneading. His hands worked mechanically, moving through well-established patterns, freeing his attention for his son. "So," he said, at last, "are you going to tell me what the matter is or will I have to pry it out of you with a serving spoon?"

Bhalon looked perplexed. "Bu' ye said to wait until the Knittin' Circle—"

"Not your quest, son," Svellin said abruptly, whacking the dough back down onto the counter and reaching beneath it to pull a handful of green onions and a long knife from the shelves below. "What's the matter with you? I haven't seen you this nervous since you broke your mother's favourite vase when you were seven years old!" Svellin began to chop the onions quickly, but finely, his eyes never leaving his son.

Bhalon's mouth opened and closed again, the normally quick-witted cleric at a complete loss for words. Lack of memories aside, he couldn't bring himself to lie to his father. Something in Svellin's calm earthiness made it impossible. "Wha' would ye' say if I told ye' I could no' remember anythin' from before I started adventurin'?" Bhalon asked.

"I'd say you must have taken a sizeable blow to the head," Svellin replied with a grin, dumping the onions and a small dish of garlic into the bowl, and grabbing a grater from where it hung on a hook above his head. That mirth faded slowly as he took in Bhalon's serious face. "When you say 'nothing' son, you mean…"

"No' you, no' mother, no' my childhood, or even m' best friend, apparently," Bhalon said in a rush, unable to hold the words back now that they were flowing. "Nothin' bu' an idea of where I came from, and a vague understandin' of wha' tha' means."

Tears crept out from the corners of Svellin's eyes and he rushed around the counter to sweep Bhalon into another bone-crushing hug. "Oh, son." When he finally drew back, Svellin's face and Bhalon's shirt were both damp. "My brave boy," he said softly, squeezing his son's shoulder. "I can't imagine how hard this must be for you. How did it happen? Was it actually a blow to the head? That's what addled your great-grandfather's wits."

"I honestly do no' know," Bhalon replied. "One day, no' long ago, i' twas pointed out ta' me. I did no' even realize my pas' t'was missin' before then."

Svellin walked slowly back around the counter, clearly deep in thought, and over to another small stone cupboard. He pulled a large wedge of cheese from it, and returned to the counter to begin grating. Bhalon waited in silence while his father finished grating the cheese and began to knead it, the onions, and the garlic, into the dough.

"Dark magic," Svellin said with a sigh, "or the gods themselves.

What else could it be? But could one of the High Lord's chosen be touched in such a way?"

Bhalon leaned back contemplatively against the wall behind him. "I do no' believe so. Dark magic may attack me directly, o' course, but no' corrupt my mind."

"Then it must be the gods," Svellin said, "or some force equally powerful. Would your High Lord allow another's god's touch on you?"

Bhalon shrugged. "As long as the touch was helpful, or benign, I suppose, but I am no' unfamiliar with the touch o' a god. I should ha' felt somethin'. Anythin'."

"Tharmekhûl forges as he sees fit, my son." Svellin finished shaping the dough into a large ball and tucked it into a small niche, on top of a piece of parchment. "Though why may be beyond us." Svellin's fingers drummed softly on the counter, as though already missing their work. "Sertig's beard!" he said, suddenly. "You won't remember how the Knitting Circle works then, will you?"

"I know they make the decisions for the kinsfolk," Bhalon said. "The king is a figurehead, and no' even he would challenge the Circle."

"Well, you're not wrong," Svellin replied, "but there's more to it than that. The important thing to remember is—"

"Master Bhalon!" a voice screeched, preceding a gangly, young dwarf (if any dwarf could be said to be gangly) by a solid few seconds. When the speaker finally came into view, all Bhalon could make of him was a seeming whirlwind of dark hair, mischievous eyes, and too-skinny limbs. "Master Bhalon!" the boy repeated, "the Circle calls!"

"Jus'ta moment," Bhalon replied tersely. "What's the one thing ta remember?" he asked Svellin.

"No time for that now," Svellin replied. "You don't want to keep the Circle waiting!"

"But it could be important, could it no'?" Bhalon said, almost frantically. "Ye said i' tis the important thing ta remember!"

Svellin waved his hands dismissively. "No time, son. Go!"

Bhalon felt himself whisked away, as though carried, by a stripling dwarf that couldn't weigh more than one of his own legs. The boy led him through a series of what Bhalon guessed were back corridors, though it was hard to tell in a subterranean cavern. The halls were barely wide enough for two dwarves to walk side-by-side, and there were few sun tubes or torches to speak of. The boy seemed quiet, almost solemn, despite his frantic introduction, but Bhalon was too deep in his own thoughts to mind.

It was a heady brew to swallow: a blood sorcerer, gods' interference, and now meeting his own parents for what seemed like first time. It was the last that made Bhalon's heart lurch in his chest. He yearned to remember the childhood that flitted just beyond his mind's grasp. Svellin was everything he could have hoped to find in a father—clearly kind and patient, but strong and fierce in his own way, as well; his arms seemed to bear as many scars of battle as they did burns from the ovens. More than stepping onto kinsfolk lands, more than walking through the stone halls of the mountain, Svellin made Bhalon feel like he had found home.

The young dwarf stopped at a set of heavy, oaken doors that looked like they could be defended for a month with no more than a bar on the inside. Steel studs the size of Bhalon's fist dotted the wood, and the hardest knock Bhalon's guide could muster was absorbed as though into the surrounding stone. Someone must have been waiting for the sound, though, as the door pulled opened silently—almost certainly on some sort of counter-weight—to reveal a hooded figure in white.

"Master Bhalon has heard the call of the Circle," Bhalon's guide said formally, his sombre tone spoiled by a crack in his voice.

The hooded figure nodded, gesturing for Bhalon to enter. The cleric's young guide slipped back into the maze of corridors without so much as another high-pitched squeak.

The ceilings of the massive hall arched so high above that they were lost in the darkness; it was a room built for majesty and awe, a room to inspire supplication and obedience. The sharp tread of Bhalon's boots on the hard slate floor seemed to disappear the moment it sounded, crushed from existence by a complete lack of echo. And yet, a soft clicking carried through the air, as though right beside his ear, reminding Bhalon of the massive scorpion's chittering. As he grew closer to the centre of the room, Bhalon realized that it was not the sounds of an animal; it was the unceasing rattle of a dozen knitting needles, working almost in unison.

The hooded guide led Bhalon down a long series of steps, toward a slightly raised dais at the centre of the room, where it would be the focal point for every one of what Bhalon guessed must be at least ten thousand seats. In the centre of the dais, spread in a half-circle facing him, nine women sat, birch baskets full of spun wool beside each rocking chair, and needles working in each pair of hands in different knits, purls, and patterns. Only one set of eyes watched his approach: a sturdy, dark-haired woman whose only concession to middle age seemed to be a few stray silver threads in her hair. Her expression was intelligent and curious, though somewhat aloof and foreboding. She was clearly the leader of the Circle, even to the most casual observer. She watched him move to the foot of the dais, which was only a hand shorter than he, forcing him to take a step back to keep them all in view. The woman stared at him in silence for a few moments, though her needles continued clicking and knitted threads flowed out like a stream of water. Bhalon struggled not to twist and fidget like a schoolboy caught dipping a girl's hair into an inkwell.

"Bhalon…Lightbringer," she said finally. "Welcome home. It's been a long time."

"Thank ye. I—"

"Your father has been very worried, you know. You could have at least sent a letter to let him know you were still alive." Her needles clicked furiously, and a grey-haired woman at the Circle's edge glanced toward her.

"Mara," the woman chided softly.

The dark-haired woman, Mara, Bhalon assumed, blushed slightly and slowed her needles, but her eyes remained hard. "Kinsfolk are expected to remain in contact when they venture outside of kin lands. You should remember that much from your upbringing. What is it that brings you back now, Lightbringer-born-Marasson?"

Well-prepared words died on Bhalon's lips. 'Marasson.' Mara's son. He met his mother's eyes, and his entire being screamed, torn between the need to find the words he needed to explain his mission, and the desire to give up completely in the face of the situation's utter strangeness and run from the room. "I seek the wisdom o' the Circle," he managed in a hoarse croak, "on a matter o' some urgency. I come to ye, callin' both as a dwarf of the Dragonstooth Kinsfolk, and as a cleric o' the High Lord."

The eyes of every woman in the Circle rose from her work in unison, unwavering as owls'. "Go on," Mara said.

"An evil tide rises," Bhalon said, starting to get his confidence back. "A sorcerer o' such power tha' the rock beneath us all shudders a' his passage, and threatens ta fracture.

An older dwarven woman, knitting what looked to be a pair of purple socks, scoffed loudly. "The kinsfolk have seen many tyrants come and go, mages, sorcerers, fools. The younger races have always been impetuous and foolish. Let them war, and this sorcerer will be overcome like all the others."

"Perhaps tha' was true in tha past," Bhalon acknowledged. "This is diffcrent."

Purple Socks laughed. "So the young always think, as though everything you see has just come into existence because you've seen it. What does a babe know but its own fingers and toes?" A few other grey heads nodded with her words.

"And how many o' those sorcerers and tyrants raised demons ta fight on their side?" Bhalon demanded.

Purple Socks finished a stich and dropped her hands and knitting into her lap with a sigh. "A few, even in my time, insolent child. The gods always sort things out before too long—they don't like anyone reaching beyond the veil they have put in place."

"And what if one had the power ta challenge the gods?" Bhalon asked softly.

"Don't be foolish," Purple Socks began. "No one has the power—"

"What exactly do you mean, Bhalon?" Mara interrupted.

Bhalon met her eyes. "He has an amulet, stolen from a barbarian I met. I'twas powerful enough ta take the barbarian from bein' able to string naught bu' a sentence or two together to seein' and hearin' the gods speak. With the amulet in hand, the sorcerer's power may well be limitless."

The Circle discussed Bhalon's words in a series of sharp, silent glares and micro expressions. A sharp-faced older woman, two hundred if she was a day and with skin that looked stretched too tightly over her bones, looked up from the green throw blanket she had been knitting with needles as big around as Bhalon's thumb. "What are the other kingdoms doing about this?" she demanded.

"Belakeer and Adana are already under his control. He has used sorcery ta usurp the existin' rulers and ta' their places, travellin' quickly between the kingdoms by way o' blood magic. My party intercepted one o' the bone fragments he's been using ta' travel, but no doubt he's sent another."

"Perhaps we should deprive him of his bones, then," Mara said darkly.

"What resistance do you propose we join, then?" Green Blanket asked. "Why should the kinsfolk form a vanguard to protect the world of men?"

"Ye will no' be alone," Bhalon replied. "Work has begun ta rouse the underground—all the thieves' guilds will unite to push back against the sorcerer's rule. An emissary has also been sent ta the orcs for their assistance; their numbers are e'en greater than those o' the kinsfolk."

"Orcs and thieves?" Purple Socks spat incredulously. "The orcs couldn't agree on the colour of the sun, and the thieves would as soon stab *your* back as any other. No, Lightbringer; this is not our fight."

"That is not your decision to make, Terellee," Mara snapped. "It is the Circle's."

Terellee was irritated enough that she dropped her purple socks down into her lap. "Don't be absurd, Mara. We're not going to march the kinsfolk to battle—alone—against a superior force on one man's word, no matter who he is. You're letting your emotions get ahead of your duties."

"How dare you accuse me of putting anything ahead of the kinsfolk's good!"

Terellee scoffed. "And it's not the first time, either, letting Svellin task kinsfolk messengers with asking about your son in the outer world, exposing them to any danger his foolishness might have gotten him into!"

Silver light had begun to leak from beneath Bhalon's fingernails and he could feel the same warm light seeping from the corners of his eyes and the hollows of his ears. "Ladies," Bhalon said imploringly.

The Circle ignored him, intent on what looked to be an impending fist (or worse—a knitting needle) fight between two of its members.

"—this from the woman who was bedding Larne Teresason when she was supposed to be deciding Circle business not a month back!" Mara screeched.

"Ladies!" Bhalon called again, but it was no use. He watched the silver light flow over the flesh of his hands moments before his vision disappeared.

"Circle of the Dragonstooth Kinsfolk!" The words shook the massive hall, the Voice of the High Lord bursting forth from Bhalon's lips. Silvery light flooded from Bhalon's body, illuminating every corner of the hall, while waves of echo brought crashing silence behind them. Had a ball of wool dropped from one of the Circle's baskets at that moment, its fall would have seemed loud as a clash of arms in the newfound quiet. "Such actions do not become the stoic courage and fortitude with which Tharmekhûl imbued thee. It has ever been the granite resolve of thy kind to stand against the evils of this world, and assist its champions."

The Circle exchanged guilty glances.

"My cleric comes to thee not just as a man, but as my voice. My words are Truth. Leave aside thy petty squabbles. Take up thine arms. Let the wicked fear the ceaseless tread of the dwarves."

Bhalon's vision returned slowly, as though he had stared too long at a torch. The silver light withdrew, leaving him feeling empty, but still suffused with the love of his god. There was the lingering sensation of a gentle hand on his head, and then Bhalon stood alone again before the Circle.

Green Blanket picked up her needles, and gentle clicking began again. "Well, Terellee, I'd say that answers the question, wouldn't you?"

Mara's full-throated laugh filled the room, as comforting and warm a touch for Bhalon as the High Lord's own hand. "Would anyone else of the Circle like to debate the point, or can we call that decided?" More needles resumed clicking, but no voice broached the silence. "There you have it, then, Bhalon. The dwarves will march."

Bhalon smiled broadly. "Wonderful! My thanks ta ya Circle, and—"

"Just a moment," Mara said softly, her eyes still intent on her son. "There is still the matter of payment to discuss."

"Payment? Wha' payment would the Circle ask o' the High Lord?"

"Oh, no, my son. We would never ask payment from Him. I speak of payment from *you*."

Bhalon's mouth hung agape, and a feeling of dread washed over him at the look in his mother's eyes. "And wha' would ya ask o' the High Lord's *cleric*, then?"

Mara's smile was predatory. "Again, nothing. I wouldn't dream of interfering with a cleric's calling. Of Bhalon Marasson, however, the Circle would ask a price. Anala!"

Anala, out of her armour and dressed in simple grey, woolen breeches and a green knitted sweater, climbed onto the platform from the rear, where she had clearly been waiting to be called. She strode to the side of Mara's chair. "Yes, Knitter?"

"How long have you known Bhalon?"

"We were born within a month of each other, Knitter. I have known him my entire life."

"And what is your estimate of him, as a dwarf?"

Anala looked taken aback. "He was a mischievous boy, but a good-hearted one, I think. He has ever been a dependable friend, and he's chosen by the High Lord himself; I don't think it's our role to criticize His chosen."

"I didn't ask you to criticize the High Lord's chosen; I asked you to critique a dwarf and kinsfolk. Why do you think he has never married?"

"Knitter?" Anala asked, clearly startled. Bhalon felt a cold sweat break out at the small of his back.

"Marriage, Anala. You do know what that is, do you not? Why do you think Bhalon hasn't yet married?"

"I don't know, Knitter. I suppose, his calling…and his time away."

"Would he make a good husband?"

Anala's eyes widened, and her mouth opened and closed silently. Mara sat back patiently, her needles clicking while Anala tried to find her voice.

Bhalon felt as though his leg had been caught in a bear trap. If he had believed for a second that chopping off his foot would have helped, the limb would have flown in an instant. His eyes met Anala's.

"I expect he would," Anala said, at last.

Bhalon had to admit that Anala was attractive, at least. Her woolen sweater couldn't hide her broad shoulders, nor could her breeches hide her wide hips and shapely legs. But marriage? He had never even considered marriage before—had he?

"Have you, or any others you know, chosen Bhalon?"

"No, Knitter."

Mara's voice was gentle. "Would you do so now, child?"

Bhalon was surprised at the small hurt he felt at Anala's firm tone: "no, Knitter. Bhalon is my friend, but only my friend."

"Thank you, child. Would you go and get Masel Norasdotter, please? I believe you'll find her waiting in the passage."

"Yes, Knitter," Anala said, with obvious relief. She made her way quickly down the stairs and past Bhalon, grabbing his shoulder on the way by.

"Wha' tis the meanin' o' all this?" Bhalon asked thickly. "Wha' exactly is't to *the Circle* if I am married, or no'?"

Mara met his furious eyes with an icy calm. "You have asked the dwarves to leave their lands and fight a war that is not their own, for the betterment of all. It is only fitting that you offer something to benefit the dwarves, in return."

"Codswallop!" Bhalon spat. "Ye had no idea what boon I would ask o' the clan, and yet ye just happen t'have a bride waitin' in the hall!"

Mara smiled thinly. "She has been a guest in this hall for some months, while we waited for you to return home. I would have already been introducing the two of you, as your mother, and as Voice of the Dragonstooth Knitters' Circle. Now you have a good reason to say yes."

Bhalon looked around the Circle. All were busily studying their needles, and most had small smirks on their faces. "And if I refuse?"

"We will, of course, not go against the High Lord's wishes. The Dragonstooth Kinfolk will march forward to meet the sorcerer. The other clans, however…Well, who knows what decisions they might make on their own? Or if they would even find out. I'm not sure we have any messengers available to travel right now, and I imagine you're eager to get back to your little group."

Bhalon, his face a thunderhead, sought within for the feeling of his god, and found only the barest hint of gentle laughter. Seeing that amusement mirrored on his mother's face only further enraged him.

Two sets of footsteps, one the confident stride of a warrior, the other a soft, hesitant patter, made their way down the steps and into the room. Bhalon turned to find Anala leading another dwarf with her— presumably Masel Norasdotter. As they approached, Bhalon felt his pulse rise and his mouth go dry. The girl was tall for a dwarf, standing at least a hand above Anala, and long, golden hair rained down her shoulders and back. She was slim of waist, surprisingly long of leg, with delicately-boned hands and cheekbones that sat high below wide eyes. She was, in a word, hideous.

"Masel," Mara said, "be welcome to the hall of the Dragonstooth Kinsfolk. This is my son, Bhalon."

Masel bowed deeply to the circle. "Greetings, Circle, from the Ironsforge Kinsfolk." She turned to Bhalon, looking him over with a clinical detachment—a horse trader judging a new stud. She smiled briefly. "Hello, Bhalon Marasson, called Lightbringer."

Masel had a strength of voice that seemed unlikely from so delicate a frame. Somewhere in it, Bhalon found the power to reply. "Greetings, Masel Norasdotter."

"I understand that you have a proposal for me, and for the Ironsforge Kin," Masel said briskly.

Bhalon froze, tongue-tied, but it was Mara who answered. "Indeed. The Circle proposes a marriage between you and my son, Bhalon. As you can see, he is whole in body, and mentally well. He is also a cleric of the High Lord, as you are aware. The terms of marriage are to bond the two kinsfolk. The Dragonstooth Kin would receive preferential trading with the Ironsforge, particularly your tools and weapons—"

"—With an equal preference to the Ironsforge Kin for Dragonstooth livestock and clothing, of course," Masel added.

"Of course. Our whole livestock and knitted wear—"

"—and your meat products and woolen felts, as well, naturally."

Mara grinned wolfishly. "Agreed, provided that we also receive preference for your raw iron and armour. You, my dear, will make a very interesting daughter-in-law."

Masel smiled faintly at the praise. Bhalon felt his stomach plunge.

"Time is short," Mara said, "and we have agreements to sign, and a marriage to plan. Bhalon, why don't you go see what your father is doing?"

With a frown like a thunderhead, Bhalon, cleric of the High Lord, and son of the Dragonstooth Kinsfolk's Voice, walked out of the room, doing his best not stomp his feet like an angry child.

CHAPTER 4

OF FATHERS AND DAUGHTERS

Giselle grunted in disgust as her right foot squelched ankle-deep in the slick mud. Filthy water flowed into the few remaining dry spots of her boot, after a long day of walking through the muck and quagmire that made up the South Haraxian swamps. A lizard-lion as long as a horse slithered along the banks of a deeper water course to Giselle's right. She met its predatory gaze with a look equally flat and violent until it turned and splashed back into the brackish waters.

Gods, how she hated this place! There was a reason (alright, more than one, perhaps) that she had left this cesspool behind her.

Bracing herself on the firmer ground beneath her left foot, Giselle pulled her boot free with a wet pop and moved carefully back toward the center of the path. Her stockings squished wetly on her feet, chaffing her heels, but her destination was nearly in sight, and Giselle couldn't help but smile at the thought of seeing her father and brothers again. Her father would gently chide her for how long she had been away, Druskar would joke and take her out to get drunk at the earliest opportunity. Throsken, who she still saw in her mind as a gangly 14 year old tripping over the haft of his lochaber axe every time he turned, while insisting that it was the only proper weapon for an orcish warrior, would have undergone his ritual blooding to become a full member of the tribe during the months she had been away. He still had the axe, too, as far as she knew—assuming he hadn't given it up for something more sensible. What good is a weapon too big to swing indoors?

A low snuffling from Giselle's left caught her attention only seconds before a pondstrider broke from the marsh and shuffled toward her. Nearly the size of a bear, and making similar sounds, the pondstrider moved remarkably quickly with its stocky legs and broad body; through some miracle of nature or magic, the animal's front feet, broad, shiny, and flat on their bottoms, skated across the surface of the mud and quagmire, propelled by long, almost flippered rear feet. This particular pondstrider was moving at top speed, mud and filthy water fanning up from the sides of its feet, onto its flank, and slipping easily off of the brownish-green bristles that covered its body in a covering as tight and waterproof as any duck's feathers.

Spotting her, the pondstrider launched itself forward. The soft snuffling turned into deep grunts, blown past a mouthful of teeth that put even its natural lizard-lion prey to shame. As it drew near, Giselle tried to throw herself out of the beast's way. It pivoted quickly, it's rear feet cutting into the muddy ground like rudders, and struck her square in the chest, knocking both of them back into the muck.

The pondstrider brought its face inches from Giselle's, lips drawn back and teeth bared.

"Hellfire, Trump! Get off of me!"

The pondstrider continued to grin happily down at Giselle, snuffling at her face and armour.

"Trump!" a deep voice boomed from further up the path. "Where in the nine hells have you gotten to now? I swear, if you have your head stuck in that hollow tree again, I'm leaving you there!" A tall, slender orc burst out of the bushes, a collar and lead hanging from his hands. He moved with a thoughtless grace in impeccable cream-coloured trousers that showed not a speck of mud, despite the bog around him. His face showed some of the same fine bones as Giselle's, but with skin closer to the colour of a ripe avocado. He let out a full-throated whoop when he saw Giselle, plunging forward to grab hold of the loose skin on the back of the pondstrider's neck and pull him back off of Giselle.

Giselle fought to remain stony faced. "Your pondstrider nearly drowned me, mudsucker."

"Then I suppose you should have stayed out of his way, swamp witch."

They stared at each other in silence for a moment before the slender orc's composure broke and he flashed a broad grin that showed fangs slimmer than Giselle's own, but a full two finger-widths longer. "Welcome home, sister." He took her hand and levered her up out of the mud before folding her in a tight embrace. "It's good to see you."

"You too, Druskar. It's been too long. How are father and Throsken? How fares the kingdom?"

The smile faded from Druskar's face. "It's good you've returned. We need you here."

"That well?" Giselle asked.

A ghost of a smile twitched across Druskar's lip. "Worse, probably. Come on; let's get you back to the castle and cleaned up. I'll stay with you until father can see you."

"Watching my back?" Giselle asked.

"Yes," Druskar said, flatly. "The quicker you get cleaned up and back into arms and armour, the better." He turned and began walking briskly back along the muddy path leading to the fortress.

"If it's so dangerous," Giselle said, "why are you out here along, and basically unarmed?"

Druskar gave Trump a scratch on his bristly back. The pondstrider leaned into the scratch and let out a grunt of pleasure. "I'm hardly alone, and I trust Trump more than anyone else in the palace—except you and father, of course. Nor am I unarmed," he said, reaching behind his back to find the hilt of a rapier.

Giselle raised an eyebrow. "And what would you possibly do with that, Brother? Spear flies? Roast meat? Throsken must never let you hear the end of it."

Druskar frowned. "No. He doesn't. Throsken doesn't hold back much of any criticism these days."

Giselle stopped walking. "What's going on, Druskar? No more cryptic answers."

"But those are the ones I'm best at," Druskar said. "It can't be that bad, if we can still poke fun at it, right?" He sighed. "Throsken has joined the Young Bloods."

Giselle growled, deep in her chest. "Has he lost his bloody mind? His father is the Nalrag! He can't be part of a tribes-first group; it's treason!"

"It's been a bit tricky to get around, I'll admit," Druskar said.

"A bit difficult?" Giselle demanded. "That stupid ass!"

"You're going to frighten Trump if you keep yelling like that."

"Trump is too stupid to be afraid," Giselle said. "You're just changing the subject."

Druskar grinned. "It's that or have the entire kingdom show up to see what you're yelling about. I know you're a mighty adventurer now, and all, but I'm not sure I'm quite ready to help you take on all the rebels before lunch."

"Blobwyrm," Giselle said, affectionately.

"Hagfish."

They started down the path once more. The slippery mire was slowly giving way to gravel and packed earth, and the castle edged into view. More fort than castle, the structure still closely resembled the motte and bailey construction from which it had grown; two central circles still dominated the design, with the smaller one, raised up onto higher ground, surrounding the main keep where chieftains, priests, and blacksmiths primarily lived. The wall defining the circle had been broken in half a dozen places over the last decade, as ease of moving people and products slowly became more important than fortifying an inner perimeter. The outer circle, now a stone wall, rather than the original wooden one, protected most of the craftsmen and warriors of the various clans now living under one "roof." Camps sprawled out around the walls unevenly, housing more warriors and crofters wherever the land remained dry enough to permit it.

As they got within hailing distance of the walls, Druskar slowed. "He'll try to provoke you, Giselle. Or he'll have one of his friends do it. Don't lose your temper. And don't do anything stupid."

Giselle put her hand on her brother's shoulder and gave him a winning smile. "When have I ever lost my temper?"

Druskar burst into laughter.

*　　*　　*

The throne room of B'Haratruk, Nalrag of the orcish peoples, was, perhaps, a little underwhelming. Where a petitioner might expect to see troll skulls lining the walls, racks of heavy iron weapons, and wooden floors stained from bloody coups, they found instead shelves of books, piles of scrolls, and a large wooden desk with a heavy wooden chair— more an administrator's office than a king's throne room. Torches lit the windowless room, aided by a branch of candles on the desk, next to the Nalrag himself.

When Giselle and Druskar opened the heavy wooden door, B'Haratruk looked up at them blankly for a moment, his mind returning slowly from the stories told by the papers in front of him. "Welcome home, daughter. As always, you show up just when I need you most." He pushed back the oaken chair and walked over to wrap Giselle in a hug. Giselle beamed, bending low to return his embrace. After a moment, B'Haratruk slacked his grip and leaned back to look her in the face, from a full head's-height below Giselle's own. "Grom's bones, but it's good to see you again," he said, his broad grin emphasizing teeth easily large enough to be considered tusks. "And looking every hair a warrior. Your mother would be so proud, Giselle."

"But not my father?"

"Nalrags are too proud, already," B'Haratruk said with a grin. He glanced down at her mud-covered armour. "Sit. You've clearly been travelling hard. Have you brought the idol with you? That may at least buy us some time with the Young Bloods."

"No, father, I didn't. I found where the thief was, but there's much more to it than we thought. It's much bigger than just Southern Haeraxa." Giselle sat in the chair across the desk from her father's, and he followed suit. Druskar remained standing, his hand on the hilt of his sword, and his eyes shifting between the two doorways to the room.

"Giselle, we've been over this before. Let the humans do what they will. It's naught to do with us. The swamps will protect us, as they always have."

Giselle shook her head. "And you're as wrong about that as you've ever been. Did the swamps keep the idol safe?"

B'Haratruk grimaced. "A swamp can't protect you from a lizard-lion."

"What do you mean?"

"The sorcerer had help in getting the idol out of the keep," he said grimly. "The same help that's now trying to take my throne."

"Ogrimm's tusks!" Giselle said. "If things are so unstable, why are you mobilizing to the north? I know the idol is important, but—"

"The idol is worthless dross!" B'Haratruk bellowed.

Druskar jumped, a foot of blade clearing his scabbard, as he carefully watched the doors. Finally, convinced they were alone and unheard, he let out an explosive breath. "I know that Doomhammer once said 'all orcs must die,' father, but I would greatly prefer it not be today!"

B'Haratruk opened his mouth, an angry retort on his lips, but he seemed to think better of it and nodded grimly. "I have not set the clans toward the north, though the Young Bloods have been pushing for it, and spreading rumours in neighbouring kingdoms. They are using the loss of the idol as evidence that I am unfit to rule. Whether or not that cursed piece of bone every belonged to Rah'Ost Skullcrusher or not, he was the last orc to unite the clans, and it doesn't look favourable if I cannot even keep a memento of him safe. How then can I hope to lead, as he did?" He ran a hand across his face exhaustedly.

Giselle was uncomfortably aware of how old her father was, by orcish standards—especially for a king or clan leader, nearly all of whom were fated to lose a blood challenge when age began to take the strength from their limbs.

"Don't look at me like that, daughter," B'Haratruk said, as though reading her mind. "I could still take you and your brothers together, if I had to." His grin faltered and they sat in a grim silence for a moment.

"Why?" Giselle asked. "Why has Throsken turned against us?"

B'Haratruk lifted his hand to his face, caught the movement, and firmly put his arm down on the desk again. "Power. What else? He knows I would never endorse him as a successor—he's never had the brains or the temperament to rule—and he's decided he would rather be a clan leader in a fractured kingdom than a faithful vassal in a whole one."

"But we're his family!" Giselle said.

"When has that ever meant anything to him?" Druskar asked softly, his eyes never leaving the hall's doors.

B'Haratruk sighed. "It was better with your mother around. She would have made him see sense, even if it meant teaching it to him with her fists. She'd have managed it, too."

"I miss her," all three said at once.

They sat in silence for a moment, lost in memory. At last, B'Haratruk cleared his throat. "Enough of that," he said gently. "We have other things to worry about here and now, without wishing for a past we can't have back. I think it's safe to assume that we're not going to get the idol back anytime soon. If you couldn't find it, daughter, the sorcerer has almost certainly had time to take it far enough away and hidden it well enough that we won't find it now."

"I agree. That's why we need to focus on the coming war. We need to begin mobilizing. Now."

"Not possible. It's exactly the opportunity the Young Bloods need. They've already been sowing seeds of rumour and lies, trying to discredit me and sway the chieftains away from my rule. If I send armies without going myself, I will be dismissed as a weakling. If I go with the armies, there will be nothing to come home to."

"Why not have them killed?" Giselle asked, bluntly.

B'Haratruk frowned. "Leaving aside the fact that I would rather not have to order the death of my own son, it's simply too late. Attacking them openly now, after they've had the chance to pour honey in the ears of the chieftains, would lead to exactly what the Young Bloods hope to accomplish, anyway. The only option left is to try to hold things together."

"If we don't move soon, it's not going to matter if we can hold things together here. The sorcerer will come for us."

"And the swamps will protect us."

"No, father. Not this time. They're already failing us, and all he has had to do is take an old hunk of bone. How much worse will he do once he's built his power in the other realms?"

"Which realms?"

Giselle shrugged. "All of them, I think. He's already made himself king in Belakeer. We suspect he's done the same, or soon will, in Adana, though Baron Nahwell."

B'Haratruk spat. "The filth. How is it that Belakeer hasn't revolted? They loved their king."

"Because they don't know that anything has changed. The sorcerer uses blood magic to change his shape; the king's own brother wouldn't know the difference."

"By the prophet's tusks," B'Haratruk said.

"How do you know all of this?" Druskar asked.

"The mage I was travelling with figured it out, when we captured a piece of the sorcerer's little finger being taken to Adana."

"Blood magic," B'Haratruk said in disgust.

"You've always hated magic," Druskar said. "What were you doing travelling with a mage?"

"Perhaps I should start at the beginning," Giselle said.

"Indeed," B'Haratruk said, "but not before you've had a chance to clean up and change. I'm not entirely without manners, though Druskar may not agree on that." He turned to his son. "Go with her. Watch her back. We'll dine in our family quarters when she's cleaned up."

*　　*　　*

Druskar stood outside the sole entrance to the bathing room while Giselle washed in the shallow trough of tepid water that passed as a bathtub in the keep. The trough was clean, at least, as so few orcs bothered to use it in the first place.

As Giselle wiped the mud and road grime from her emerald skin, she pondered the little she had learned from her father. It was hardly surprising to find out that the Young Bloods were challenging her father's rule; that was simply what the tribes did, under one name or another. They had warred so long and so fiercely amongst themselves that only the strongest leaders could unite them—and then only temporarily. What Giselle couldn't accept was her own brother's role in trying to overthrow her father. To be fair, that wasn't exactly unheard of, either; more often than not, it was the son of the chief, or the son of a former chief, demanding the blood challenge. But she couldn't help but remember Throsken as a toddler, catching rats with his bare hands (and teeth); as a pestering eight-year-old that she could always goad into ridiculous situations; or as a teenager, hauling around an axe far too large for him and doing his best to be a 'true orc.' When had her brother grown up, and how did he become such a cave troll?

She squeezed grit and brown water from her cloth, sluicing it around in the trough for a moment before starting in on her arms and legs. The pond muck had dried on like a carapace, which Giselle supposed made her a bug of some kind. She laughed softly, in spite of herself, at the ridiculous picture that came to mind of her with long feelers sticking out of her forehead.

She was belting on the leather armour a servant had brought for her to wear when Druskar knocked softly at the door.

"Giselle?"

"Come in. I'm nearly done," Giselle said, pulling on a hardened leather bracer and beginning to pile her armour into a carriable bundle. "Do I have time to wash out my padding?" she asked, eyeing the heap of rust-stained, sweat-infused cloth pads that normally sat between her skin and the abrasive iron of her plate armour.

"I'd like to get back to father," Druskar said, shortly. "Leave the padding for one of the servants. Bring your plate, though; you can always buckle it on over the leather, if you have to."

Giselle picked up the heavy, awkward bundle of armour from the bench, shifting it to find a balance point. Druskar smiled faintly, but didn't offer to help, his eyes turning back to the corridor, and his hand on the hilt of his sword.

"I'm surprised you're not carrying it unsheathed," Giselle said. "Is it really so bad?"

Druskar's eyes met hers. "Worse. Come. We should get back to father. Your homecoming may spur some of the stupider Young Bloods into doing something...stupid."

They spent the rest of the walk in silence, stopping as they neared the non-descript oak door that led to their family quarters. In front of the door, stooped with age, but armoured and armed as a warrior, stood a white-haired orc that grinned at them through enormous, pitted, yellow teeth.

"Little bird," the old orc grated, his voice gravelly and tired. "Welcome home."

Giselle smiled, shoving her pile of armour into Druskar's hands so that she could pull the old orc into a rough embrace. "Valdroth! Are you still alive?"

Valdroth chuckled deep in his chest, his eyes sparkling behind enormous white eyebrows. "How could I die before I've made my way through all of the castle maids?"

Giselle gave him a mocking, flat stare. "I thought you'd managed that already when Druskar and I were still orclings. Ogrimm knows, we caught you with them often enough."

Valdroth grinned again. "True, but there are always maids leaving and new ones starting, and I move a little slower than I used to."

Giselle shook her head, smiling affectionately. "You old boar."

"For the right sow."

Druskar cleared his throat, nodding toward the door. "We'd best get in there, before father wears through the floor with his pacing. You two can make fun of each other later."

"Always was a bit of a prick, wasn't he?" Valdroth asked Giselle, opening to door to let them through. "We'll have a drink and catch up later, little bird."

B'Haratruk was, indeed, pacing slowly before the large stone heath, the blazing fire throwing his silhouette toward the door. His twin swords lay unsheathed on the long table, somewhat out of place with the meal simmering in the stone crocks and earthenware dishes laid out for their meal. The Nalrag's short legs stopped as his children entered, closing the door behind them.

"What kept you?" He glowered at Druskar. "And what were you going to do if attacked? Hit them with your sister's breastplate?"

Druskar flexed his jaw, but said nothing, piling Giselle's armour on a side table before coming to sit at the table opposite Giselle. B'Haratruk took the seat at the table's head, motioning them to fill their plates.

"I can fight my own battles, father," Giselle said, spooning spiced meat and tubers onto her plate. "And Druskar was only holding my armour so that I could greet Valdroth properly."

B'Haratruck grunted. "He deserves the greeting, I suppose. It's quite the situation when the only orcs I trust are two of my own children, and a servant—a warrior from another clan."

Giselle laughed. "Father, you captured Valdroth more than twenty years ago. He's lived nearly as long as your servant as he did a warrior of the Pythons. He practically raised us after mother died."

"That's true enough, I suppose. I was so busy trying to unite the clans by then…"

"We know," Druskar said. "It's fine, father."

B'Haratruk shrugged. "It is what it is. Now, daughter: you were going to start at the beginning, you said."

Giselle nodded, swallowing a mouthful of spiced vegetables that left her mouth tingling. "I did. After the sorcerer fled with the idol, I tracked him as best I could. His trail disappeared almost immediately, but I had no idea how. Finally, I gave up on the trail itself, and headed toward Belakeer, as I thought that was where he was most likely to end up."

"Given how he wanted us to harass their border, you were probably right."

"I was, but I couldn't get near him. Every time I thought I had tracked him to his hiding spot, he would vanish—even in Shimano. The one time I caught him out in a public square, but he had enough thugs with him to distract me while he escaped again. I finally managed to capture one of the men I thought he was using as a messenger. He told me about a package the sorcerer was sending to Morath—some sort of important bone, or relic. I guessed that it had to be the idol, so I paid the messenger to stay quiet and waited for the sorcerer to send out his envoys to Morath. Then I followed them."

Giselle paused for another bite and a swallow of ale. "Naturally, the sorcerer had done something to hide their trail—at least for the first part of the journey. I hunted them through southern Belakeer, and back into the northern forests of Haeraxa, and finally picked up a solid trail. The trouble was, there was someone else trailing them, who I thought must be mercenary reinforcements—a rear guard to discourage pursuit."

"What sort of group?" Druskar asked around a mouthful of bread and well-aged cheese, drizzled with shalrak, a traditional mixture of rancid oils and fermented bitters.

"Mixed. A dwarven cleric that I took for a warrior, a mage, a ranger, and…a barbarian."

B'Haratruk raised an eyebrow at the way Giselle paused over 'barbarian,' but said nothing.

"I decided I had to eliminate them before catching up with the messengers, or I would risk losing the trail, or having them catch up at the wrong time. I tried to ambush them, thinking it would even the odds enough, but it didn't quite work out that way."

"Only four of them?" Druskar said. "I've seen you take on as many as six, in training."

"Training is not real battle," B'Haratruk reproved.

"They weren't really standard warriors, either," Giselle said. "The barbarian was a tougher foe than expected, and I hadn't realized that the dwarf was a cleric. He used some sort of magic to get behind me while I was focused on keeping the barbarian between me, the mage, and the ranger."

"Did they take you to the sorcerer, then?" B'Haratruk asked.

"No. They were tracking the envoys, as well, trying to capture them, so they brought me along."

"That seems awfully trusting," Druskar said.

"Well, there were some magical chains involved," Giselle said. "At least, in the beginning. After we caught up to the envoys, the sorcerer took over the envoy, and the group needed my help to defeat a monster that he raised."

"What was it?" Druskar asked.

"And more importantly, how did the sorcerer raise it, if he wasn't there?"

"I think they call it a stinging crab in the northern deserts, but much bigger. Its head was level with my own, and its tail could have topped our castle wall."

Druskar whistled appreciatively.

"The cleric and the mage said that it was blood magic. The bone the envoys carried was a part of the sorcerer's finger, not Skullcrusher's arm."

"Ogrimm's teeth! And you managed to defeat a beast, raised through blood?"

"Yes, father. The group I met is…formidable. They're not just average adventurers."

"Clearly not, if you're so taken with the barbarian."

Giselle's face warmed, and it wasn't just the spices. "I never said I had an interest in Grug."

"Grug, is it?" B'Haratruk said. "You didn't have to say it. I know you, my daughter."

Giselle raised her chin defiantly. "And will you try to forbid it?"

B'Haratruk laughed. "Try? I'm not so great a fool as to try to lift the moon—and far be it from me to tell any child of mine who to love. Follow your heart, Giselle. Just don't let it overtake your head."

"What's he like, this Grug?" Druskar asked. "And why was his party chasing after the sorcerer's envoys?"

"For the same reason I was. The sorcerer stole something from them—from Grug, actually. An amulet. With it…well, it's hard to explain, exactly." She took another mouthful of meat, chewing slowly as she thought. "It's clear that whoever holds it becomes more intelligent—much more intelligent. Grug claims he can…hear the gods."

B'Haratruk and Druskar looked at her in uncomfortable silence.

"He's not mad," Giselle said defensively. "He may be the most grounded man I've ever met."

"So then, the sorcerer wants the amulet to commune with the gods?" Druskar ventured.

"No. He wants to dethrone them."

"Hellscream's axes," B'Haratruk cursed softly. "That this should come on me now, when the strength in my limbs has begun to fade." He blew a deep breath and met his children's eyes. "And so your barbarian goes to war, and you wish the orcs to go with him."

"Yes."

"We shall."

"But father," Druskar said, "the Young Bloods. We'll either have to wrestle them away from our allies at every turn, or leave them here and come home to a broken kingdom."

"Then so be it, my son. The tribes have been broken and reforged before. We can't allow the sorcerer this victory. If he can truly challenge the gods, what pitiful defense can the orcs mount against him, even in our swamps? As for the Young Bloods—"

The door crashed open, the heavy wood thudding into the wall behind it. Throsken strode in, his lochaber axe held easily on his right shoulder, and an arrogant smile on his face. Giselle could see two other young orcs behind Throsken in the hall, holding Valdroth, one with a knife pressed to the old orc's side. Another two orcs stood in the hall, with their weapons drawn.

"Am I no longer invited to family dinners?" Throsken boomed, with false humour. "Or to greet my own sister upon her return home?"

"You're always welcome, if you're prepared to be respectful, my son," B'Haratruk said coldly, his eyes seething.

Throsken smiled, leaned his axe against the end of the table, and grabbed a slice of bread from a platter. "I'm always respectful of those that deserve it, old man." He turned a chair around and straddled it, chewing loudly and with his mouth open. "So, sister. Returned with Skullcrusher's idol, have you? Ready to pull us all back together into one big happy family?"

Giselle glared silently at her younger brother.

"Aww. No luck? Did daddy's little pet fail? A truly sad day."

"You can be civil, or you can get out," said Druskar venomously.

"Don't worry, brother," Throsken said. "I take no more pleasure being here than you do having me." He threw down what was left of his bread. "I invoke the right of blood challenge, B'Haratruk."

Giselle shot to her feet, her chair clattering to the ground behind her. "Throsken, no! Don't be a fool."

"I'm not a fool!" Throken roared, surging to his feet with axe already in hand, his eyes wide in crazed fury.

Druskar stood, slowly and deliberately drawing his sword, the steel rasping against the wood of the scabbard. "Get out."

"I have invoked blood challenge. I—"

"I will stand as father's champion," Druskar said emotionlessly. "You're welcome to try me any time."

"No," B'Haratruk said quietly. "I will allow no champion."

"But father—"

"I said 'no,' Druskar. This is my challenge to meet, and I will do so." He looked at Throsken. "We will carry out the challenge tomorrow at noon, in the fighting pit. Now get out of my sight."

"Or what?" Throskan said defiantly.

"Or I will have you removed."

Throken smirked. "The last I looked, there were five of us, and three of you. Maybe I'll just take care of a few blood challenges all at once."

B'Haratruk smiled grimly. "I think you may have miscounted, son. What's your count, Valdroth?"

The young orc holding a knife on Valdroth had let his blade drift as he watched the exchange between Throsken and his family. At B'Haratruk's call, the aging guard's hand shot down, trapping the young orc's wrist and the blade in his hand. Bone broke with a meaty pop and the young orc squealed in pain. Valdroth continued his turn with unexpected speed, grabbing the other orc next to him by the forehead and driving his skull back into the stone wall.

Valdroth pulled curved twin blades, each as long as Giselle's forearm, from behind each hip and gave the two remaining orcs in the hall a flat-eyed stare. "I make it four to three, B'Hara," he said mildly. "But I could make that four to one, if you'd rather."

B'Haratruk hadn't taken his eyes off of his youngest son. "You want to be a 'true orc,' Throsken, but you have no idea what that means. Skullcrusher and Doomhammer would be shamed by your actions.

A fleeting spasm of pain crossed Throsken's face, but it was quickly replaced by anger. "A true orc is victorious," he said. "I will crush you in the pit tomorrow." He turned on his heel, the haft of his axe clattering against a table leg, and stormed from the room. His pair of cronies followed, carefully staying out of Valdroth's reach.

"No, my son," B'Haratruk whispered softly. "A true orc fights and dies with honour."

CHAPTER 5

BLOOD FROM A STONE

When the wall first began to shimmer, Grug thought it must be a trick of the fading light. As the spot grew, he wondered if he had lost his mind. When the spot was a little higher than Grug's waist, and only slightly wider, fingers began to emerge, followed shortly by toes, near where the wall met the floor.

"Crom!" Grug yelled, throwing himself against the back wall, as far as possible from the spot now sprouting forearms and knees. As the barbarian watched in shock and amazement, the disparate pieces resolved themselves into the stocky figure of Gnarrinshang Shalevelkin, his eyes closed, and a resonant humming coming from his bare, bony chest.

As the last bit of his heel emerged from the stone and touched down on the floor of the filthy cell, the deep humming stopped and the gnome's dark eyes opened. His broad, flat teeth gleamed in the faint light as he smiled at Grug, and he strode, somewhat unsteadily, to stand in front of the barbarian. "Is good you are alive," Shalevelkin said. "Friends will be pleased." He smiled again, and tottered on his feet.

"Shalevelkin okay?" Grug asked. "Seem...shaky."

The gnome waved away his concern. "Fine. Passing through stone..." he hummed for a moment, trying to find the word. "Too healthy. Stone too pure. Makes..." he waggled his hand. "Fine soon.

Need to leave now."

Grug held up his hands, the heavy, iron shackles clacking loudly. "Guard has key."

Shalevelkin shook his head dismissively, putting his bony hands over each manacle and humming in a much higher pitch than he had before. After a moment, he gave a sharp pull, and the cuffs shattered, leaving red powder caking the welts and scrapes that covered Grug's wrists. The gnarrinshang repeated his work on each of the shackles ensnaring Grug's ankles.

Grug rubbed gently as his blood-encrusted wrists, wincing as some of the scabs broke open. "Thank you," he said simply.

"Welcome," the gnome said, with another smile. "Come. Must go." Turning on his heel, and seeming steadier than before, Shalevelkin marched back to the wall. "When go through," he said, turning back to Grug, "do not let go. Will get stuck."

"Stuck?"

"Stuck."

"Okay." Grug took two steps toward the gnome before his brain erupted in flames—or so it seemed to him. He fell to his knees, an agonized roar bursting from between his teeth and his wide, bloodshot eyes bulging from their sockets.

Shalevelkin turned back to Grug in surprise. "Nedross!" the gnome swore. "Grug? What is it that happens?"

Grug's eyes focused on the small figure before him, and he coiled to leap forward, his hands clenching murderously. The leap never came. With a wet, slopping sound, Grug's back leg plunged into the stone floor up to his thigh. In the blink of an eye, the stone solidified again, leaving the barbarian fastened securely in the rock and awkwardly stretched on its surface. He bellowed his rage again, as Shalevelkin studied him, carefully out of reach.

Locks rattled heavily from the hall, and the jailer burst into the room, a short club already in his hand. "What the bloody hell is going on here?" he said.

Shalevelkin made a deep, resonant, grunting sound, and waved his hand dismissively, without ever taking his eyes off of where Grug was struggling mindlessly toward him. The jailer disappeared into the floor, as though he had stepped onto the surface of a lake.

The gnarrinshang continued to peer at Grug, muttering and chittering softly to himself as the barbarian gnashed his teeth and railed against the implacable hold of the stone. His eyes finally found the cut on Grug's forehead, partially hidden in the greasy mess of his black hair. "Segojan's gem!" he cursed. "Blood magic." He moved inches beyond Grug's grasping fingers, watching for patterns in the big man's movements. The next time Grug's hand pulled back and moved toward him again, Shalevelkin exploded forward, his left hand twisting and locking the barbarian's wrist while he spun closer, reaching up to grab the back of Grug's neck—which was thankfully much closer to the floor than it would have normally been. The gnome continued his spin, shoving Grug's head down into the suddenly liquid stone.

Grug thrashed as though drowning beneath the surface of the grey floor, but Shalevelkin held him firmly, droning in an angry buzz. As the barbarian's flailing slowed, Shalevelkin pulled him up and peered into his eyes while Grug drew a wracking breath. Shaking his head, the gnome plunged Grug back into the stone again for the space of a few breaths and tried again. Satisfied, he slid Grug onto the surface of the floor, Grug's muscled body suddenly buoyant in the pool of liquid stone.

The barbarian panted and retched. "What gnome do?"

"Blood magic took mind. Put into stone."

"Will it come back?"

The gnarrinshang shook his head slowly. "No. Stone too strong. Take much more power than even sorcerer has. Can walk?"

Grug nodded shakily. "Yes," he said hoarsely, pushing himself to his feet.

Shalevelkin approached the wall again, already humming, and pressed his fingertips into the stone. "Hold. Tight."

Grug bent down behind the gnome and crossed his arms over Shalevelkin's chest. In a moment, he had been pulled forward, into, and through the stone. Grug closed his eyes tightly and held his newly-caught breath while he and the gnarrinshang passed through the very grains of the stone, which crawled like ants on Grug's skin.

The room they emerged in was dark, and Grug could smell the faint scent of rotting vegetables and cured meats. Shalevelkin said nothing, gently pulling Grug's arms away from his chest and taking the barbarian's left wrist to lead him through the darkness and toward the outline of a door.

The corridor in which they emerged was long and poorly lit—a servants' corridor, for moving about the business of the castle without offending the delicate eyes of the nobility. The gnarrinshang staggered, slightly glassy-eyed, a few steps ahead of Grug, talking quietly to himself in gnomish and stifling an occasional giggle. His sense of direction, or his memory of the passages, was uncanny, however; though each stone corridor seemed to branch into the next seemingly identical two or three, Shalevelkin confidently led the way from one to the other, passing by storerooms and the occasional empty hall. Finally, he opened one of the many identical doors and led Grug through a storeroom smelling of pitch to a rough-hewn wall, made up of much larger stones than those used in the interior of the castle.

"Is here," Shalevelkin said. "But will be difficult."

"Why?" Grug asked.

"Outer wall. As thick as Grug is tall. Is also vishlecktilas...you would call granite. Tight grain. Will take long to pass. Don't breathe."

Grug grunted. "Why not use courtyard?"

Shalevelkin shook his head. "Too many guards since tried to steal amulet, and would still need to get out of gate, or go over wall."

He took a deep breath and placed one hand on the stone. To Grug's senses, Shalevelkin seemed to grow more solid, as solid as the wall itself, with each angle of his body growing more stark—from the broad expanse of the gnome's jaw to the sharp protrusions of his elbows. The colour of his skin faded, from the shade of a walnut to a deeper, sandy grey—nearly the same as the stone he touched.

"Come," Shalevelkin said.

Grug once again pulled himself against the gnome's back, enfolding him in his arms and taking a deep, gasping breath as he neared the surface of the wall. Then he was within. His previous journey through the stone of his cell had been quick enough that Grug barely had time to feel the stone around him. Now he felt as though the entire weight of a mountain was crushing him—as it swallowed him whole. He couldn't even have said that he was drowning, for the stone didn't flow into his lungs. He simply couldn't empty, nor fill them again. He didn't dare to open his eyes.

Shalevelkin moved forward as though walking through deep water, his muscles quivering as they pushed against the resistance of the stone. Grug held on, trying not to crush the gnome as panic took a firmer and firmer grip on him. The seconds stretched, and Grug began to see stars. He knew his panic was probably making it harder for Shalevelkin, but every fiber of his being screamed for him to claw his way out of the stone.

Then he felt the night air.

First his hands, and the arms grasping Shalevelkin's chest, then, blessedly, his face. The yell that would surely have burst out of him came out instead as a surprised grunt, as the gnome pitched forward, with Grug sprawling on top of him. Grug hastily rolled off of the gnome and rolled him over. Shalevelkin was breathing, but clearly unconscious, his lips split in a silly grin, even as he slept.

Peering into the night to make sure they hadn't been noticed, Grug gently picked Shalevelkin up from the ground, cradling him to his chest, and jogged quietly into the dark alleyways of Shimano.

CHAPTER 6

ROCK YOU LIKE A HURRICANE

The soil of the fighting pits was rocky and black, the colour coming as much from the elements themselves as from the blood spilled in an endless series of feuds between members of warring clans, and members of normally peaceful clans...and arguments between members of the same clan. Despite the solid ground in the pits, the smell of the swamp was never far away, and a cloud of gas and insects rode the wind currents around the gathered orcs.

Giselle, in painstakingly-cleaned plate armour, stood with her father, brother, and Valdroth, the smell of hot iron and sweat drawing more than her share of mosquitos—though clearly frustrated ones, for the most part. Valdroth bore his own heavy plate without complaint or concession to his age, while Druskar and B'Haratruk sweated in chainmail and boiled leather more suitable to their lighter frames and speed. As was tradition, only B'Haratruk was armed, the rest having left their weapons at the pit's entrance to limit interference in the duel.

Across the pit, Throsken stood with five of his cronies--two more than tradition normally called for. All wore orcish war armour, a mixture of cuirass, chain mail, greaves, and gauntlets, all painted garishly with blood and decorated with bones of enemies they had slain. Giselle couldn't help but note that Throsken's armour was decidedly bare compared to his companions, but the look on his face said that he was prepared to add new decorations, no matter what the cost.

Giselle turned back to watch her father work through his loosening-up exercises. Despite his age, he moved well, though the clean, unadorned armour he wore stood out, when compared with Throsken's friends'. "Father, I wish you would have worn your bones."

B'Haratruk glanced up at her from where he was stretching out his short legs. "You know how I feel about that, Giselle. Every bone is--"

"--another orc you've failed to win over with logic. I know, father, but *they* don't understand that," she said, motioning to the orcs now ringing the pit to witness the duel.

"And that's why we must continue to educate them," B'Haratruk responded calmly.

Giselle sighed exasperatedly. "You know them, father. They only respect power. You--"

"No, Giselle. Don't ever make that mistake. They *fear* power—even their own. They don't respect it."

Druskar laughed humourlessly. "You're saying that the clans spend their entire lives chasing something they're afraid of?"

B'Haratruk grinned mischievously at his son. "And now the two of you know precisely why it's so difficult to lead, and to hold the clans together. We crave power, but every time we grasp it, it burns us. Together, we are strong enough to take any of the lands on the continent. But that same strength consumes us from the inside. Like a moth that finally gets to the flame it desires, we burn brightly for a moment, and then die spectacularly when the same power that drew us together, splits us apart. The clans disperse again, far enough from each other to limit the killing, and we wait for the next leader."

B'Haratruk climbed to his feet and began stretching his chest, back, and shoulders.

"Then wearing your bones would show you can grasp that power, wouldn't it?" Druskar asked.

"No, son. Wearing the bones shows that I am being consumed by it."

"The only way to show you can lead, is to lead," Valdroth rasped.

B'Haratruk smiled broadly at his old friend, tusks gaping. "You have been listening to my rambling all these years, then."

Valdroth grinned back. "It took a long time for the words to burrow their way in, but be damned if I could get rid of them once they got there."

B'Haratruk stepped forward, clasping wrists with Valdroth. "It has been my honour to have you with me." He stared into the other orc's eyes. "Take care of them, if I fall."

Valdroth swelled visibly, becoming taller and more menacing. "Always."

B'Haratruk turned to Droskar, pulling his son into a hug, his head resting uncomfortably on his son's leather cuirass. He pulled back and put one hand on Druskar's shoulder, staring proudly into his eyes, as though all the words of importance had been said. Druskar gave his father a rare smile and squeezed his shoulder in return.

When B'Haratruk turned to Giselle, his eyes were already shining.

"Enough!" Giselle said, with a laugh. "You're going into a two-minute duel, at best, father."

B'Haratruk laughed, but pulled his daughter close, bringing her head down to his own temple. "Part of me will die today, my daughter," he said softly. "Even if everything goes according to plan." He pulled his head back to look her in the eyes. "Lead them."

When he stepped into the centre of the pit, B'Haratruk was a different man. He bristled with menace, a short sword, matched well to his height, in each hand. His footing was sure, his body almost languid in its grace; he was a panther, stalking its prey. Light glinted off of his blades as he continued warming up with his weapons, alternating between slow control and blurring speed.

Giselle looked across the pit to her brother and saw fear on his face, the look of a boy led by his own pride to a place he now worried he would never leave. Around him, the rest of the Young Bloods jeered at B'Haratruk, baring fangs and twisting their broad chests so that their bones clacked together like macabre wind chimes.

Unable to help herself, Giselle walked around the pit's edge. One of the Young Bloods moved forward to bar her way. He was as tall as Giselle, but carried himself woodenly, as though he believed that his heavy footsteps and bulked shoulders could make him more formidable.

His mouth hung open, his breathing heavy, and his breath terrible. "Get back to your side, crow fodder," he said, spattering Giselle with spit in his effort to simultaneously bare his fangs and form words.

Before Giselle could reply, Throsken stepped forward, putting a hand on the other orc's chest and pushing him back. His axe gleamed in his other hand, the long handle touching the ground. "You shouldn't be here. It's against tradition. They could kill you, without even starting a feud."

"You don't have to do this, Throsken."

For a moment, his eyes softened and Giselle could see her little brother in the cold face of the warrior before her. "I have to do what's right, Giselle. I have to do my duty as a true orc." He began to turn away.

"You stubborn ass!" Giselle said. "There's more to this than pride. Can't you see they're using you?"

The orcs behind Throsken began to push forward as one, growling low in their chests. Throsken roared back at them, halting their advance. He rounded on Giselle. "I do what must be done," he yelled. "I do it for all of our honour, while you chase worthless baubles and our father makes all of us weak through his endless words of unity, without the tusks to take the fight to our enemies. We deserve better!"

"That's those idiots talking, not you! Use your brain, Throsken! Is an army weaker or stronger because it has both archers and infantry? Are you more afraid of one lizard-lion, or a swamp full of them?"

Thosken faltered a moment in the face of her logic. "You must have been too long with humans, Giselle," he said at last. "Their ways are not our ways; their truth is not our truth."

"Spoken like a fool. There are only truth and lies. You've clearly been fed too much of one to taste the other."

Throsken's face contorted as it had when he was a child, about to have a tantrum. "I am a true orc!" he bellowed, with the orcs behind him roaring in response. "I will not be told how to act by any…human lover!"

Giselle had a moment of confusion as her mind turned to Grug. She felt a brief flush of shame that was immediately consumed by anger. It took every ounce of self control that she had not to lash out at her brother, to make him hurt for the shame that now coloured her feelings. When she had mastered herself again, she spoke softly. "Goodbye, brother. We love you. Can you say the same of them?" She spun on her heel and began marching back toward Druskar and Valdroth, unwilling to let Throsken see the tears now making their way slowly down her cheeks.

Druskar watched her approach, his eyes sad and sympathetic.

"How the hell did it get this far, Druskar?" Giselle demanded, her voice quiet enough not to carry across the pit. "I've only been gone a few months."

Druskar shook his head slowly. "Giselle, you're fooling yourself if you think this only started after you left."

B'Haratruk, a light sheen of sweat on his face, rejoined them while Throsken took to the centre of the pit, warming up his shoulders with broad sweeps of his axe. "Throsken has been a member of the Young Bloods for at least three years, daughter. Perhaps longer, but not by much. The rest of them thought he was a joke, or perhaps a poorly-chosen spy. Since he took his warrior's rites, it's been different. They realized what kind of power he had given them. Legitimacy."

"And he could finally deliver a blood challenge," Druskar added, "once he'd passed through the rites."

B'Haratruk blew a sigh and let his blades drop back to his sides. "Indeed. All of the responsibilities of a warrior, and none of the experience."

"I'd have told him where that leads, if he'd asked," Valdroth said gruffly, but with a small smile on his lips.

B'Haratruk barked a sharp, surprised laugh, but the mirth was short-lived; his face fell back almost immediately into the set, strained expression he had worn since entering the pit.

"If we could just—" Giselle began. Her mouth snapped shut, biting off the end of her words, as the priests of Bhagtru appeared from the shadows of the castle doorway and made their way slowly around the fighting pit. The head priest, his robes a deep crimson, made his way slowly, and with dignity, into the centre of the pit. Mordeth was older than B'Haratruk by at least twenty winters, and covered in a vast network of scars—a small handful of which still looked to be healing.

Bhagtru was a harsh master, and theological disagreements were most frequently settled by knife fight. Giselle didn't know how refined Mordeth's theology was, but his skill with a blade was legend before she had even been born.

The high priest quelled the last murmurs of conversation with a glance of his hazel, almost yellow, eyes. Though his face was impassive, serene, those eyes promised the swift justice of Bhagtru to any that challenged the priest's authority…or spoke out of turn…or looked at Mordeth in a way he didn't like.

"Warriors of Bhagtru," Mordeth intoned, "we bear witness today to a blood challenge between B'Haratruk and Throsken, of the Mosquito Clan, spoken and accepted in the presence of witnesses. Do either of you wish to deny or recant it?"

B'Haratruk shook his head briskly. Throsken bared his teeth.

"Bhagtru approves of your challenge, and will accept the blood of your sacrifice. You will fight to the death, or a crippling. The winner may take bones."

B'Haratruk's lip lifted in a grimace. The five orcs accompanying Throsken leered and stroked the bones sewn to their armour.

"Treachery," Mordeth continued, the word rolling from lips twisted like he had sipped vinegar, "will be punished by the gods." He gestured around the fighting pit, where priests had silently joined the crowd at even intervals. "The punishment will be administered by their priests— and it will not be swift." His eyes measured Giselle, Druskar, Valdroth, and each of Throsken's five, in turn.

Mordeth turned his gaze to B'Haratruk. "As Nalrag of our people, you may choose your second, and your Nal-Eth—your choice of successor, if they are strong enough to hold it, should you fall."

B'Haratruk answered without hesitation. "Giselle is my Nal-Eth. Druskar will stand as my second."

Giselle's eyes bulged in surprise, but she knew better than to interrupt the High Priest. Druskar caught sight of the look on her face and quickly stifled a laugh.

"Challenger," Mordeth said formally, "choose your second."

"Naspur," Throsken said shortly, gesturing to one of the orcs around him. Naspur, a broad-shouldered warrior with crosshatched bones on his chest, and a matching pattern of tattoos on his face, raised his arms as though he had won a great victory and flashed his tusks in a wide grin.

"As the challenged, you have the right to choose weapons," Mordeth said.

"Fighter's choice," B'Haratruk replied. "I will wield dual swords." He bowed shortly to the High Priest over his crossed blades.

"I will fight with an axe," Throsken blurted out, before B'Haratruk had even completed his bow, "the true orcish weapon." He raised his lochaber above his head, its long haft still only feet above the ground.

The High Priest scoffed. "A true orc can use any weapon to bring death, pup. We will discuss your theology later—if you survive this day."

Thosken lowered his axe, crestfallen, a chastised child—which, Giselle realized a moment later, he still was. The stupidity of the situation threatened to overwhelm her for a moment, leaving her shaking with impotent rage. Druskar put a hand on her forearm and squeezed gently.

Mordeth had made his way back off to the side of the fighting pit. "Fight with honour," he boomed. "Begin!"

Giselle had expected Throsken to rush in, whirling his axe and bellowing a war cry. To her surprise, her brother calmly raised the head of his axe over his right shoulder, ready to swing vertically or horizontally, and began a patient, measured, advance.

B'Haratruk crouched lower, in a knife fighter's stance, with his left blade held out in front of him, and his right drawn close to his side. He waited, coiled like an adder, and almost supernaturally still.

The pits were as silent as a tomb—so quiet that Giselle could clearly hear the crunch of gravel, sand, and stones beneath her brother's feet. As Throsken came near striking range with his long axe, Giselle watched for the telltale shifting of his left shoulder that would signal the beginning of his swing. Instead, Throsken surprised her again, beginning his swing by stepping back with his left foot and bring the axe down, almost gently, across his body, twisting his right hip to add speed and force to the heavy blade. It was a defensive move as much as an aggressive one, using mobility of both head and haft of his heavy weapon to form both a weapon and a shield from B'Haratruck's smaller, much quicker blades.

As Throsken slowly advanced, his axe whirling, both head and haft blurring, B'Haratruk gave ground, his feet shifting back and to the side in a wide circle; he was clearly waiting. What he was waiting for soon became apparent. The muscles of Throsken's torso twisted and surged with his movements, and sweat was already trickling down his cheeks. B'Haratruk watched impassively, drawing Throsken ever forward with his own slow retreat.

The moment was short, the mistake so minor, that most of the crowd missed it. B'Haratruk did not. As the head of the axe flew past Throsken's left shoulder, the weight of the enormous weapon, and his gradually-tiring muscles, pulled him off balance, forcing him to move his left foot wider and twist ever so slightly to the right. The whirling haft would have left no opportunity for a less-skilled swordsman than B'Haratruk, or one wielding a heavier weapon, but the Nalrag of the orcs was both eminently skilled, and carrying weapons that let him use every ounce of his speed. His right blade flicked out gracefully as he sprang forward, caressing the outside of Throsken's left knee, parting the tendon and ligaments with near-surgical precision. B'Haratruk scuttled back as his son dropped to his knee, screeching in pain, and narrowly avoiding the head of his own axe, as it whirled past his face and crashed into the ground in front of him.

In a blink, B'Haratruk was next to Throsken, his left foot pinning the axe to the stones, while his right blade, already accented with crimson, targeted his son's throat. "Yield."

Giselle watched Throsken's face move from pain, to panic, and into stubborn resolve. "No. Finish it."

"Damn it, boy! Yield!"

"Death first!"

Giselle felt the impact of the first, long black arrow, as though it had struck her own chest. The weight of the impact knocked B'Haratruk back a few paces, and he stared at the shaft in surprise.

Mordeth was already moving when the second arrow hit B'Haratuck, spinning him around and knocking him to the dirt. Knives emerged from the High Priest's cassock and took flight, slapping into the belly of a black-masked figure in a second-floor window of the castle. Throsken's supporters surged forward to where Throsken knelt on the sands of the pit, stunned and staring at the still figure of his father. Naspur pulled a dagger from where it had been hidden beneath his cuirass and strode toward to B'Haratruk's prone form.

Druskar launched himself at B'Haratruk, grabbing for the hafts of his father's swords. Giselle dug her toes into the gravel and sand, her legs straining to propel her fully-armoured body forward. Her face wore a mask of pain and anger that would have made a Fury proud, and a guttural roar burst from her lips as she crashed into Naspur, knocking him off of his feet and sprawling back onto the sands. Giselle threw herself on top of him and rained down blows with her gauntleted fists.

Her mind was a haze, shrouded in rage. She struck Naspur again and again, breaking teeth and tusks, long after he had lost consciousness. She sank her teeth into a green forearm that tried to wrap around her neck and pull her off of the other orc. The warrior behind her screamed and fell back, a sizeable chunk of flesh missing and bright blood covering them both in red mist.

When Giselle finally regained her feet, the fight was nearly over. Druskar was pulling one of B'Haratruk's blades free from the chest of one adversary, with a second lying still not far away. Mordeth had a long knife in each hand, and the one in his right fist was stained with gore that matched the disemboweled orc screaming on the ground in front of him. As Giselle watched, the last of Throsken's retinue turned and fled toward the castle entrance, only to be felled by a practiced cast from the High Priest. The warrior fell with a squawk, as the impact of the blade knocked the air from his lungs. Only Throsken and B'Haratruk lay where they had fallen when the fight began, like a horrible tableau. Throsken's eyes were wide with shock and his pupils dilated with pain. Giselle ignored him for the moment and moved toward her father, only to be stopped by Mordeth. "Not here. We must get you inside."

Giselle bared her teeth at him, battle lust and a cry of pain entangling at the back of her throat. Mordeth grabbed her shoulder and looked deep into her eyes. "You are your father's Nal-Eth. There are bigger things at stake than your love for him."

Giselle held his eyes for a moment, fighting for self control, then she nodded tersely. The High Priest motioned to the handful of priests that had materialized around them, some with red-tipped knives of their own. They were broad, scarred orcs, all, but they knelt down and picked up B'Haratruk's body with the gentleness of a mother with her infant. Giselle and Druskar shared a long look before they walked over to their brother and lifted him from beneath either arm. Throsken cried out in pain as they shifted his leg, but said nothing.

*　　*　　*

When the three siblings entered their father's office, the priests had already laid B'Haratruk's body out on his long, wooden desk. Valdroth stood guard at B'Haratruk's side, as he always had. Mordeth shoed the lesser priests from the room, and motioned to Throsken. "Take him with you. Do what you can for his leg." Two of the priests obediently lifted Throsken and bore him from the room.

Mordeth followed the priests, closing the door behind them, and securing the bolt with a snap.

Giselle jumped. "What's going on, Mordeth?"

"Something best dealt with in private, Giselle," Valdroth grated from behind her.

"True," B'Haratruk said wryly, swinging his legs over the edge of the table.

Giselle gaped, managing only a strangled croak.

"Bhagtru," Druskar swore, his face so pale it was nearly yellow. "How? Why?"

B'Haratruk's smile faded. "Because I would rather not kill my own son, or die to him."

Valdroth snorted. "Not much bloody chance of him winning. With the openings that little fool left you--"

B'Haratruk raised a hand, and Valdroth quieted. "Thank you for your help, Mordeth. Will your 'assassin' be alright?"

"A graze. He caught my knife's blade almost entirely in his cloak. How is your chest?"

B'Haratruk looked down at the broken-off arrow shafts sticking out

65

of his leather hauberk. "Unfortunately, I'm not as talented as your man. The lower arrow pushed through a bit."

"We'll have to work on that for next time, then," Mordeth said sarcastically.

Giselle had finally found her voice. "What in Ogrimm's name is going on?"

"I told you," B'Haratruk said calmly. "I won't kill my own son. And the Young Bloods pushed him far enough that I had no other choice—except this one." He smiled sadly at Giselle. "Besides which, I would never have been able to do what must be done. You can, though. You will."

"What?" Giselle said.

"You were his Nal-Eth," Mordeth said. "You are now Nal-Rag—if you can hold it."

"She will," B'Haratruk said confidently.

Druskar was staring at Giselle thoughtfully. "What?" she demanded.

"It's not a bad plan, actually. Father never could have led the tribes north, after refusing the Young Bloods for so long. It would have been political suicide."

"If not literal," B'Haratruk agreed.

Druskar nodded. "Probably. You, though, Giselle…You've got a chance."

"You're both crazy!"

B'Haratruk smiled. "Likely. It runs in the family, you know. I'm also right about this. Of that, I have no doubt."

"Let's assume you're right—just for a moment," Giselle said. "Why me? Druskar—"

"Not a chance," Druskar said harshly. "You're not putting this on me. I'll follow you; I'll watch your back; and I'll defend you to the edge of the world, but I won't take this from you. I wouldn't last one turn of the glass before I decided to kill half of those idiots father has spent years bringing onside. I might make them fear me by the end, but they'd never respect me."

"They'd also drive a dagger into his back the first chance they got," B'Haratruk added. "I told you I'm in no mood to lose one of my children."

"And what makes you think I'll do any better?" Giselle asked.

Druskar shrugged. "You always have, Giselle. Even when we were small, you could always get away with things I couldn't. Hell, half the time, Throsken and I would even get away without a thrashing, if we let you do the talking. Do you remember the time that we nicked all of those new blades by pretending the posts in the forge were an invading army? I thought the bladesmith would have the skins off of our backs, until you started talking."

"What can I say? I've always been the charming one."

"It's more than charming, you cave troll, and you know it! By the end, you had him convinced that we were doing our duty as orcs, preparing to keep our homeland safe. He'd have followed you into battle, with you all of nine years old."

"Likely still would," Valdroth said. "He still asks after you, wants to be sure you're well and doing great things."

"The clans will follow you, Giselle," B'Haratruk said. "They just couldn't do it with me here."

"And what will you do, then? Live on a farm somewhere and raise sheep?"

B'Haratruk laughed. "Not quite. I'll stay in hiding until the clan chiefs have sworn to you. Then I'll join the priesthood. Mordeth has promised to show me some new tricks with a knife."

"Then why all of this?" Giselle asked. "Why not just step aside and join the priesthood openly?"

"Because when a chief steps aside willingly, he can't name a Nal-Eth," Mordeth said. "It has ever been so. Only a chief that has named a successor before falling in battle has the right to name even a temporary successor. Besides, even if he was openly a priest, there are those who would see him as a loose end to be cut away."

"More importantly, daughter, we don't have time for a civil war at the moment. You're a wonderful leader, Giselle, but orcs have been known to ignore good sense and compelling words from time to time. Becoming Nal-Eth lends you legitimacy—a crack that you can prise against."

Giselle sighed deeply and leaned back again the desk beside her father. "Alright. I give up. I'll do it. Now what's next?"

Mordeth smiled wickedly. "Now we plan a funeral."

*　　*　　*

Giselle watched her father from the corner of her eye, and wondered what it was like to attend your own funeral. B'Haratruk, veiled in formal priest's robes and boosted slightly in tall boots, stood with the other priests of Bhagtru. He even stood differently, holding his shoulders at a different angle, just in case. Even Giselle wouldn't have recognized him, had she not known where he would be standing. And he was lucky to be standing, she thought irritably. She hated sitting in full plate; it chaffed and pushed in odd places. Still it was better to have it and not need it than to need it and not have it—today, of all days.

Druskar, sitting next to her and looking significantly more comfortable in his leather and mail, leaned over to whisper in Giselle's ear: "where did they find a body that matched that well?"

Giselle glanced at the granite altar, on which a shrouded body lay. Even from where she sat in the front row of the temple, she would have sworn it was B'Haratruk's body, had she not known better. "I didn't ask. Mordeth said that as long as they found someone who looked even a little like father, he and Bhagtru could do the rest."

"But it's even the right height. What kind of luck or magic is that?"

"Neither, if I understood right," Giselle said. "It was a saw and some metal pins. Now shut up and look like a dutiful, grieving son. Even Throsken has a more somber face than you today."

Druskar looked past Giselle to the end of their row, where Throsken sat. Throsken looked like nothing so much as a kicked puppy; his leg would be months in healing, even after the ministrations of the priests, and his friends had all abandoned him immediately after his failed challenge. He had almost blubbered in happiness when Giselle and Druskar had allowed him to attend the funeral. Valdroth sat beside him, his lined face tightly controlled.

Druskar sat back, and Giselle turned her attention back to

Mordeth. The priest was actually a decent orator, his gravelly voice and scarred face commanding attention and respect on their own—though his words also bespoke a much more impressive mind than one might have expected in a man that won his position mostly through knife fighting. Though he included the canonical funeral sentiments, noting how B'Haratruk's various resilient attributes—from his bone density to his stubbornness—would make it more difficult for Bhagtru to break him down in the ever-fires of the world to be reshaped in his next life, there was a subtle subtext of unity, comparing the cohesion of the body to the unity of the orc tribes, and the sadness following the eventuality of their fracturing.

When the ceremony had concluded, Giselle and Druskar joined Mordeth at the altar to fit a full helm over the face of the orc that was not their father. Druskar placed one hand solemnly upon the body's chest before returning to his seat and leaving Giselle, as Nal-Eth, alone next to Mordeth.

The high priest turned back to the parishioners and gave the ritual cry of the bereft: "and who will take up his blades?"

Giselle took her father's twin blades from beside the body and crossed them formally in front of her before answering the priest's call. "I have his swords. Will any fool try to take them from me?"

Mordeth quirked an eyebrow at her addition of 'fool' to the traditional reply, but said nothing. The room was silent for a few moments, as though everyone was afraid that the sounds of their breathing might be taken as a challenge. Then, with a snorting grunt, an orc stood in the second row. As tall as Giselle, but wider through the shoulders, the orc bulled his way past the rest of his row and stood before Giselle. "I will take them from you. I am Tchatuk, son of Vlachuk, of the Pondstrider Clan." He turned back to the assembled orcs. "I will be your Nalrag, and I will crush—" His face took on a look of fleeting surprise, as Giselle's blades plunged upward into his back, meeting behind his breastbone.

When Giselle pulled the swords back, her hands and the hilts were slippery with blood. "I accept your challenge, and delight in the taste of your defeat. Is there another so foolish?"

This time the silence stretched on breathlessly for nearly a minute.

At last, Mordeth, the hint of a smile still clinging to his lips, took pity on the crowd. "The blades are yours, Giselle, Daughter of B'Haratruk, of the Mosquito Clan." He turned to the crowd and bellowed: "rise and swear your fealty."

The crowd surged to its feet, booming their support to the new Nalrag. Giselle watched them, her face as neutral as she could manage, as though merely accepting her due. When the orcs were silent again, she began to speak. "Mosquito Clan; Lizard-lion Clan; Python Clan; Pondstrider Clan; orcs, all: your blood is mine, and mine yours. In all of our veins runs the blood of warriors, beating through our hearts like war drums. Bhagtru made us to be this way, made us to be unstoppable when we stand as one. Ogrimm shaped us, as did my father, but it is up to us left here to decide where the deadly spear of our courage will be cast, and where our mighty axes will cleave."

Druskar felt himself being caught up, ensnared by his sister's words, and a look around the room confirmed that he certainly wasn't the only one; nearly every orc in attendance watched with a fanatic fascination.

"When our people first threw off the shackles of bloodlust, revolted against the touch of demons, and fought for our freedom, we were united for the benefit of all. When Ogrimm brought the clans together to turn back the tides of men, intent on obliterating our race, he did it to strike down evil and save us all. When the mighty Skullcrusher forged us into one arm with which to swing his axe, he did it to save our ancestral homelands from the mad attacks of Garnahral, the troll king.

"We stand at the edge of a precipice, a battle as large as any faced by orcs in the time of demons, or when Ogrimm and Skullcrusher led us. And it is more important than any of those struggles—for if we win, we will save our race; we will preserve our homeland; and we will once again drive back the same kind of blood magic that once enslaved us all. Standing shoulder to shoulder, clan to clan, we will once again find our strength, our direction. Fighting beside dwarves, elves, and men, we shall prove that the strength and power of orcs can be used for good, and we will earn their respect, as well as their fear.

"Will you stand with me?"

The roar shook the room. Druskar stood and roared with the rest of the warriors. Behind his priest's cowl, B'Haratruk felt his heart sing with pride and battle lust. The orcs would go to war.

CHAPTER 7

IN NEED OF CACHE

By the time they made it back to the thieves' den, Shalevelkin was back on his feet, though still wobbly. Marcus, who was on door duty with a wiry, but dangerous looking member of the smuggling faction, threw open the door with an uncharacteristically broad smile on his scarred face. "Welcome back," he said, clapping Grug on the shoulder. "We were afraid there might not be much left after the sorcerer got hold of you."

Grug smiled back a bit shakily, remembering the fires of blood magic in his brain. "Gnarrinshang help."

Gnarrinshang Shalevelkin shook his head. "Grug is strong. Even strongest among gnomes cannot make nedross stone bear weight."

"The guild master will be pleased to see you, anyway," Marcus said. "Come." He led them up the back stairs and through a warren of back rooms, until they reached the guild master's office.

Samuel was on his feet, almost before Grug was all the way in the door. He smiled brightly. "Welcome back, my friend!" His eyes flicked over the dried blood on Grug's forehead and wrists. "Not too much worse for the wear, I hope?" He turned to Shalevelkin, bowing deeply. "Brightly woven, Gnarrinshang. Brightly woven, indeed."

The gnome smiled, returning the bow. "Was as told, guild master. Deepest level of dungeon; right on top of stones."

"Thank the gods for that, at least."

Shalevelkin grunted in agreement. "Will go to…how would be said? Tend flock?"

"Of course. Emaflintross and Obsidialkin are downstairs. I've offered them quarters up here near the rest of us, but—"

"Not necessary," Shalevelkin said. "Both have spent most time underground. More comfortable near stone, now. How soon to meet?"

Samuel glanced over at Grug. "Let's allow our big friend here to clean up and get some rest. I would expect you might like to do the same. Perhaps we could all meet for breakfast in the board room, shortly after daybreak."

Shalevelkin nodded to the two of them, turned, and started back toward the stairs.

"Come, Grug," Samuel said. "We've a room set aside for you. You must be exhausted." He guided the barbarian through a maze of narrow hallways. After the third time Samuel had taken a right turn, almost immediately followed by a left, Grug asked: "why so many turns? Confusing."

Samuel grinned. "It's designed to be, on this level, as a way to deter intruders. Lots of false and unnecessary walls slow people down and get them turned around."

"Thieves guild afraid of thieves?"

Samuel laughed. "As odd as it may seem, yes. Thieves from other guilds, but also assassins, guards, and the occasional person who manages to figure out where we are and makes it past our door wardens—not that that happens very often."

The two finally reached a staircase, which ascended to a much more logical-looking second floor. Samuel led Grug along the outer corridor to a small room clearly kept for visitors, with a small pallet, fireplace, table, and chair. A small bronze tub, not nearly Grug's size, but still a welcome sight to the tired barbarian, occupied the centre of the room.

"I'll have some food brought up right away. Would you like the tub filled tonight, or in the morning?"

Grug's brow lowered as he thought. He was tired enough that even holding onto the threads of the conversation was becoming difficult, but the thought of climbing beneath blankets still covered with the dungeon's filth was too repulsive to bear. "Tonight," he said, "but soon."

"Fair enough, my friend. The water will be here before you're done your dinner. Sleep well, and we'll talk more in the morning."

Grug grunted his thanks and dropped onto the chair, which creaked warningly, but held. Samuel slipped quietly from the room and closed the door. Within minutes, a mousy thief appeared with a tray of food, staring at Grug with a mixture of wariness and awe. Behind him followed a procession of young thieves bearing steaming buckets. As Samuel had promised, the tub was filled by the time Grug finished eating, and he folded as much of himself into it as he could.

With the grit, sweat, and filth gone, exhaustion quickly claimed the mighty barbarian. He barely made it to the pallet before his eyes slammed closed, and oblivion overtook his senses.

*　　*　　*

The next morning dawned grey and rainy. Grug stared out the small window of his room, marvelling that it could be almost the same size as the cell he had occupied in the dungeon, and yet make him feel so differently. A soft knock at the door brought him out of his reverie. "Yes?"

The same small thief that had brought him dinner the night before opened the door and stuck his head through the opening. "Umm…Mister…Smash? The guild master sent me to tell you that everyone is gathering for breakfast in the board room. I can take you there, if you like."

Grug nodded, casting his eyes around the room to see if he had forgotten anything—though there wasn't much to forget. He felt naked not having a sword or axe with him, but he supposed that couldn't be helped at the moment. He would have to find replacements later.

The young thief led Grug back to the stairs and up to the board room. Grug noticed that some of the stains from his last visit still decorated the treads—once blood has seeped into wood, it can be difficult to scrub back out. More had changed in the board room itself. The sections of the heavy, oak table that had been hewn by weapons had been replaced with a lighter-coloured wood, leaving a pleasant alternating striped pattern to the surface. Several chairs had also been replaced, and it appeared that the guild had chosen simpler, more Spartan seating of light oak to replace the heavy, carved mahogany ones.

The collection of people around the table were even more varied than the furniture. Haeronor and Triwathon sat at one end, the mage taking the seat directly at the foot of the table. Samuel sat at the head, with Marcus to one side of him and Kolya Ministiera, pickpocket faction leader and current chair of the Council of Elders, on the other. Beside Marcus sat Gnarrinshang Shalevelkin, along with two other gnomes that Grug didn't know. The two newcomers were a sharp contrast with Shalevelkin's quiet seriousness. Their large ears sported at least ten golden hoops each, and their necks were hung with almost as many chains and jewels as they bore rings on their hands. Lounging in dark leather vests and pants, the two chittered animatedly in gnomish, laughing often and uproariously. Grug smiled and nodded at the group, grabbed a plate at the sideboard, and filled it with various breads, cheeses, and crisped meats, before seating himself next to Kolya.

"Good morning, Grug," Samuel said. "I trust you're feeling a bit better, after a good night's sleep?"

Grug nodded. "Where Giselle and Bhalon?"

"They've both gone home to gather allies. I've not yet had word, but I'm hopeful that we will soon have both dwarves and orcs at our side, as well as gnomes and elves," he said, with a nod to Shalevelkin and Haeronor.

The elven mage smiled smugly. "There will soon be more elves; I have spoken to the mages' high council, and to the elders of the Tree and Leaf order. The elvenhome will not stand on the sidelines of the battle to come.

Samuel smiled genuinely and nodded at Haeronor again. "And I thank you for that. We will certainly need the assistance. Even with all of our clans, guilds, and kinsfolk, we will be facing at least two kingdom's worth of soldiers, not to mention the sorcerer himself and whatever denizens he summons. We badly need an advantage—and I believe our friends the gnomes may have found just that for us. Gnarrinshang?"

The pompous grin faded from Haeronor's face as Shalevelkin stood. The gnarrinshang offered a shallow bow of acknowledgement to Samuel, and turned his attention to the larger group. "After Grug's amulet was stolen, gnomes began searching for replacement. Emaflintross and Obsidialkin," he said, gesturing to the two gnomes beside him, "are best…how would humans say? Smellers?"

"This power does not come to humans, that I know of," Samuel said politely, "but we might call them magic sniffers, or magic seekers, I expect."

The gnome with a large, ruby stud in its nose, chittered briefly to Shalevelkin. "Obsidialkin says 'sniffer' is closer. All may seek things. Only 'sniffers' use noses to find magic."

"Sniffers it is, then," Samuel replied. "And they sense magic items, as you did with Grug's amulet?"

Shalevelkin nodded. "Yes, but is different. Gnarrinshang may ask rock to help, to tell of gems nearby. Stone senses can be dull; time is not the same for rock, and notice less detail. Sniffers can sense directly, without help from stone."

Samuel nodded. "And I take it that they've found something."

"Yes," Shalevelkin said. "Within caves of aeberethertostizicklytosdan mountains."

Haeronor raised an eyebrow, a skeptical look on his face. "Which mountains?"

"Apologies," Shalevelkin said. "Only know the daskdisky—gnomish—name."

Samuel waved the concern aside. "We have maps we can match them on. More important is what they have found."

Shalevelkin nodded in agreement. "Deep in mountains are Dwemer ruins. Obsidialkin and Emafintross tracked scent. Large cache—"

The second gnome chittered excitedly, the fine gold chain connecting the hoops in her ears to rings in her nose and lip jingling merrily in accompaniment.

Shalevelkin nodded to her. "Emaflintross says cache more than large; biggest ever found, may be."

Haeronor's eyes glowed with avarice. "And all magical? How much of it was wearable? Were there spell foci? How much did you return with?"

Emaflintross raised a hand to silence the elf and spoke at length to Shalevelkin in gnomish.

"Cache is within ruins," Shalevelin said. "Behind doors—physical and magical. Emaflintross and Obsidialkin could not enter alone."

"So, they didn't even see this fantastic cache of unimaginable riches," Haeronor said sarcastically. "We're supposed to just accept that they…smelled…it."

The humour had evaporated from Emaflintross and Obsidialkin. They sat as still as stone, their black eyes flat and angry. Emaflintross spoke slowly and carefully, her words more guttural, deeper than before. Her eyes did not leave Haeronor.

Shalevelkin listened gravely, then turned to Haeronor. "Emaflintross demands apology, or acceptance of formal challenge."

"Demands, is it?" Haeronor said, his eyes starting to glow a faint gold. "Who do you think you are, *rockchild,* to demand anything of a mage?"

The entire room had surged to its feet at the word 'rockchild,' except for Grug, who was still trying to figure out what Haeronor was fighting about, and Triwathon, who stared at his friend with shock and disbelief.

"Hold!" Samuel demanded over the sudden cacophony. All faces turned to the guild master. "You disrespect our allies, Haeronor, and you endanger our cause."

"Allies?" Haeronor spat. "A swamp of cast-off races, led by a thief? The only hope our cause has, *human,* is the magic of your betters, and now you tell us that we must follow the noses of these bejewelled, leather-clad moles? *No!* It is too much, by Larethian!"

The room was silent for a long moment. "Get out, mage," Samuel said, his voice deadly quiet. "I withdraw the hospitality of this guild house."

"If I go, I take with me the power of the magi, and the help of the Tree and Leaf!"

"Then they are well lost!" Samuel said, furiously. "I'll not have you dividing us from within. Get out!"

Grug looked helplessly back and forth between Samuel and Haeronor, wishing Bhalon was there. Triwathon, who preferred the quiet of the forest to even other elven companionship, looked completely out of his depth.

"So be it," Haeronor said, with the finality of a death pronouncement. He stormed to the exit, stomping his feet like a child, and slammed the door. As the oak crashed into its frame, the room shook, and disappeared.

*   *   *

Grug stirred groggily, his brain trying to piece together the confused jumble his senses were providing. The room was dark and felt both close and damp. The stone beneath his face was cold, but smelled of clean earth, and what looked like the bones of a fish were frozen in the stone inches away from his face. Grug absently dragged his finger over the bumps as he waited for the world to make sense of itself again.

"Barbarian!" Giselle's voice called, a moment before a strong hand grabbed the back of his chain hauberk and hauled him halfway to his feet.

"Giselle?" Grug said, confused.

"Grug!" she yelled, loudly enough to make him wince, before dropping to her knees and hugging him around the head and shoulders as though preparing to tear them off. Then her lips were on his, her fangs, which should have made the kiss awkward, somehow fitting gently to either side of his own canine teeth. Giselle drew back, her bright, violet eyes glimmering with mischief and affection.

Around them, the rest of the party stirred, slowly finding their feet. Only Haeronor, his eyes already blazing, shot to his feet, his face twisted in anger. His head swivelled, looking at the bare cave walls around them, his eyes panicked. "No!" he shouted, stamping his foot. "I will not submit to this hell any longer!" A magic missile burst from his hand, exploding against the wall. The whole party cringed back from a small shower of rock chips.

"Have ye' gone mad, Haeronor?" Bhalon asked.

The elven mage was visibly shaking with rage. "Mad, Bhalon? Oh, yes. I was mad to have ever joined up with you and this sideshow of freaks, and I'll be condemned to the eternal flames before I spend another moment locked in this foolish fantasy." He swelled with golden fire and turned back toward the nearest cave wall.

Obsidialkin's first punch doubled the mage over, the breath bursting from his lungs. The second, a spectacular uppercut, took the mage right on the chin. The golden light winked out, and Haeronor sprawled on the floor, unconscious. Obsidialkin met Triwathan's eyes defiantly as he pulled a stone-forged knuckle cover off of his hand, but the ranger didn't utter a word.

"Wha' th'a bloody hell was tha' abou'?" Bhalon demanded.

Samuel cleared his throat. "Master Haeronor has been letting his class prejudices get ahead of him."

Bhalon rolled his eyes. "Idiot. No' terribly outta character, though." He turned and bowed deeply to the three gnomes. "Ye have my apologies, brothers, sister. Haeronor has his opinions, bu' he usually keeps 'em in check."

"Blood magic?" Grug asked.

Bhalon knelt next to the mage and put his hand on the elf's forehead. For a moment, both were bathed in a soft, silvery light. "No—though i' migh' ha' been better if i' twas. We migh' ha' been able ta root tha' out. Unfortunately, there's only so much I can do ta fix a horse's arse."

Emaflintross chittered confusedly back and forth with Shalevelkin, then let out a sharp laugh.

"Wha' I can do," Bhalon said thoughtfully, "is keep 'im calm. He migh' no' be quite as useful ta us, bu' at least he will no' be puttin' all o' us inta direct danger." He lay his hands to either side of Haeronor's head, and was once again enveloped in light. "Haeronor," he said gently. "Wake."

Haeronor's eyes opened slowly, and he had a peaceful smile on his face. "Bhalon," he said, "it's so good to see you." He sat up. "Why does my jaw hurt?"

Bhalon shared a quick look with Obsidialkin. "Ye' had a bit o' a fall, tha's all. Ye'll be alright in no time."

"Okay," Haeronor agreed complacently. He finally noticed the rest of the party standing around him. "Oh, hello. It's nice to have everyone together again, isn't it?"

Giselle, who was standing very close to Grug, and holding his hand, stifled a laugh. "It's nice to see you too, Haeronor. Now that you're…feeling better…why are we here?"

Gnarrinshang Shalevelkin looked at Giselle with surprise, as though he'd only just noticed her there. "It is that the why is known, but not the how, Giselle or Bhalon is here. Is dark magic?"

"Quite the opposite," Samuel said quickly. "We believe it to be the hand of a god. It is, in part, why we are fighting the sorcerer, as we are."

"The gods take memories?" Shalevelkin asked.

"No, my friend. We believe that he gives you yours. And mine, for that matter. Like you, I remember Emaflintross and Obsidialkin telling us of the Dwemer ruins here; I remember us planning for the journey to the Norden mountains, and I remember us descending into these caves. What I don't remember is how Bhalon, Giselle, and Haeronor came to be here with us." He nodded to Bhalon. "I daresay it's worse for the three of them, who likely remember neither how they arrived, nor why they're here."

Giselle glanced over at Grug happily. "Oh, it's not all bad."

Samuel smiled. "Perhaps not, but it may require some explanation. Triwathon, would you please get some of the rations from the packs? We might as well have something to eat while we talk." He gestured for everyone to sit down again. Only Haeronor stayed on his feet, looking around the cave with a bland interest. "Haeronor, would you care to join us?"

The mage shrugged. "Okay."

When they were all seated, and Triwathon had shared out some of the rations, Samuel gestured to Giselle. "Perhaps before we dive into why we're all here, we can get an update on where things stand with the orcs and the dwarves. Giselle, were you able to convince the Nalrag to move north?"

Giselle rolled her shoulders uncomfortably. "Not exactly."

Samuel frowned in thought, already calculating how they could make do without the orcish fighters. "So be it. We'll be short on infantry without the orcs, but—"

"Oh, the orcs are coming," Giselle said. "They will just be marching with a different Nalrag at their head. Well, a Nalragga, technically, though that title hasn't been used in a few hundred years." She paused uncomfortably. "Since the last time there was a female warchief."

The entire party gaped at her, except for Grug, who smiled and patted Giselle's knee. "Giselle will be good warchief. Smart. Strong. Beautiful."

Giselle's emerald skin blushed dark as she beamed with pride and squeezed Grug's interlaced fingers with her own.

"But your father, Giselle," Samuel protested. "I'm sorry."

"Things happened as they had to," Giselle said shortly. "I'd rather not talk about it."

"Fair enough," Samuel said. "What about you, Bhalon?"

Bhalon grimaced. "I canno' say I want ta talk about i' either," he said grimly, "bu' the Dragonstooth Kinfolk will join us, as well. I canno' promise t'other kin will come, bu' 'tis likely. The Dragonstooth circle is very…persuasive."

"My thanks to you both," Samuel said. "We'll need both dwarves and orcs before this is all over. I've reached out to the other thieves' guilds in Narran, Adana, and Varasta, as well. Not all will come, but I expect we'll see enough to be of some help. The challenge, as you know, will not be solely in matching and exceeding the sorcerer's troops— which, frankly, we haven't much hope of doing. We will also be facing his magics—and we may need near-divine assistance to have any hope of overcoming that.

"When Grug possessed the amulet, he heard what he believed to be the gods. He also became more intelligent—much more intelligent."

"Far smarter than me," Haeronor said amiably.

"Indeed," Samuel continued. "Smarter even than our mage here. We've seen what a sorcerer can do with that kind of power. Why not one of our own mages? And what of other attributes? We've all come across items that make us a little stronger, or more agile—even luckier. What if we could find items that can improve those things by the same order of magnitude that the amulet increases intelligence?"

"You'd make gods," Giselle whispered.

"Gods can no' be made!" Bhalon said irritably. "Only tha High Lord can grant such powers."

Giselle opened her mouth to argue, but Bhalon sighed and waved away her protest. "I catch y'er meanin' well enough, though. Wha' value would warriors with tha strength o' a dozen ha' on the battlefield, or archers tha' never miss. Aye, they would seem like gods, would they no'?" He gently pulled his beard as he thought the idea through. "And so now ye believe ye've found some o' these items?"

Samuel nodded. "Emaflintross and Obsidialkin are what you might call magic sniffers. They've located an old Dwemer ruin, deep in the mountains, that they say holds a large cache."

Bhalon nodded. "Tha' makes sense, though I did no' think there was a Dwemer ruin tha'd no' been plundered."

"Who were the Dwemer?" Giselle asked.

"Ancient kin ta the dwarves," Bhalon replied. "Obsessed wi' machines, they were. They'd found a way ta trap magical energies in items tha' would power their machines. If i' needed strength to perform its task, they gave i' a jewel of strength; if i' needed intelligence, i' twas given it. Tha' magical energy gave tha machines all tha power they needed ta move an' even speak."

"Where Dwemer go?" Grug asked. "Why not use items to rule?"

Bhalon shrugged. "From tha tales I was told, they preferred ta be left alone wi' their creations. They could no' use most o' wha' they made themselves; like dwarves, they were too resistant ta magic ta get much effect from their items. As for where they went, no one is quite sure. They only traded a little wi' tha peoples around 'em, so it may ha' been years b'fore anyone noticed they were gone. Some say they dispersed, and intermarried with tha Kinfolk. Others say they mined too deep and found somethin' tha' swallowed 'em in flames an' soot. Some even say tha' i' was their own creations turning on 'em, tha' they decided they did no' want ta be slaves. I do no' know the truth o' it.

"What I do know is tha' ever since they disappeared, anyone who could find their ruins has been tryin' ta haul their secrets ou' by the cartload. A handful o' their treasures would pay for the rest o'a man's life. If the tales o'their mos' powerful gems are true, and not jus' stories for wee dwarves, a handful o'them could make ya neigh-on invincible."

"But no one has ever found one of these more powerful stones?" Triwathon asked.

Bhalon shook his head. "No' tha' I know of—though where the lad's amulet," he nodded at Grug, "came from may well prove they exist. Trouble is, they were said ta be difficult and dangerous ta make—and worse, the more powerful they were—so damned few even tried ta make 'em. 'Rare' is no' even the righ' word; 'mythical' may be closer."

"Wait," Giselle said. "Let's say we do find some of these gems, and they're as powerful as you say. What happens if the machines they're in don't want to give them up?"

Bhalon grinned lopsidedly beneath his bushy red mustache and hefted his axe. "Then we mus' convince them otherwise."

CHAPTER 8

DWEMER; YOU KNOW YOU ARE A DWEMER

"Well, it certainly is a nice-looking wall," Haeronor said. "Nice, even grain of granite."

Bhalon rolled his eyes. "Thanks, Haeronor. Tha's very helpful."

"You're welcome. I like being helpful," the mage said, without a hint of sarcasm.

Bhalon turned his gaze back to the blank stone wall that blocked their way, not 100 paces from the cavern in which they'd begun. "So…" he said, turning to Obsidialkin, "was this no' supposed ta be th'entrance?"

Obsidialkin and Emaflintross chittered back and forth for a moment, then back to Shalevelkin. The Gnarrinshang listened intently for a moment, then spoke to Bhalon. "Is here, but hidden. May also be trapped."

Bhalon grunted sourly. "O' course i' may be. Well, everyone take a section o' wall. Pay most attention ta where i' joins the floor an' ceiling. We'll see if we canno' find some kind o' switch."

The group spread out, carefully running their hands over each section of wall and the floor near it. The three gnomes closed their eyes, placing their hands on the wall, and tilting their heads as though listening intently.

"Bhalon," Giselle called, after a few minutes, "what's this?"

Bhalon came over to where Giselle was looking at a boulder near the left corner of the cave, and sitting almost against the wall. "What?"

Giselle pointed into the handspan of space between boulder and wall, where a strangely artificial notch ran from underneath the boulder, back to the wall. Bhalon ran his hand around the notch, scooping some small pieces of gravel out of it. "I's a track, I think," he said. "Help me push this toward the wall."

The two strained for a moment. Grug, who had been examining the wall nearby, came over and set his shoulder against it, as well, but the rock wouldn't budge.

Bhalon frowned. "Well, mayhap I was wrong—"

"Bhalon?" Triwathon called, "does that track look anything like this?"

Bhalon, Grug, and Giselle walked over to where Triwathon was looking, near the wall's other corner. Sure enough, there was a boulder with a small, notched track leading over toward the side of the cave. Bhalon pulled his beard meditatively. "Will this one move?"

The four of them strained, but the boulder stayed in place. It was the same when the two boulders were pushed at the same time. Bhalon sighed with frustration and slowly walked back toward the center of the wall, where the three gnomes still stood, hands pressed gently against the stone. "Anythin', Shalevelkin?"

The Gnarrinshang opened his still-unfocused eyes and shook his head slowly, his brow furrowed. "Is movement behind the stone. Whirring of machines, moving parts. Like stone's voice drowned out."

"Can ya go through an' see if i' can be opened from the other side?"

Shalevelkin thought about it for a moment. "Could, but dangerous. If machines attack while emerging from stone, or while recovering, will not be able to fight back."

Bhalon sighed. "I do no' wanta put ya in danger, if we can help i'. Let's keep lookin'."

A soft musical humming was coming from the centre of the caves; Bhalon turned to find Haeronor sitting on a large, flat stone in the centre of the room, running his fingers idly over the surface of the rock and singing softly under his breath. "Have you foun' somethin' there, Haeronor?" Bhalon asked.

The mage jumped a bit in surprise. "Hmm? Oh, I just wanted a rest. Thought I'd sit for a bit."

The stocky cleric walked over to Haeronor, opening his mouth to berate him. As he grew closer, however, he was able to see the place Haeronor's fingers had pulled dust from carvings on the stone's top. "Wha's this?" He gestured for Haeronor to get off of the rock, and began blowing dust from the top of it. Shalevelkin, Emaflintross, and Obsidialkin joined him, helping clear dust away while the mage stood behind them, looking slightly irritable about losing his seat. When the last of the dust and stone chips had been cleared from the carvings, Bhalon stood back to get a look at the entire surface. "Hellfire. It's a puzzle."

Shalevelkin shook his head. "No. Is lock."

Bhalon swore. "O' course i' tis." He looked over to the two corners of the cave, and the boulders sitting along the notched tracks. "An' if I'm no' mistaken, those two stones be the latches."

Shalevelkin nodded in agreement.

Bhalon blew out a breath, his long, red beard quivering. "Well, the good news, if'n ye can call i' tha', is tha' the language o' the Dwemer and the language o' the dwarves have a lo' in common. The bad news is tha' there's damned little in the way o' words here. I's mostly pictures an' patterns." His hand traced along it. "Rain, I think tha's supposed ta be," he said, pointing to a square filled with short lines. "The swirls may ha' been sun, an' the peaks are almos' certainly mountains. I do no' know wha' the three wavy lines are, though. Nor the crossed circle. Could the curved line beneath the straigh' one mean 'under' d'ya think?"

Shalevelkin studied the pictures carefully and nodded. "Yes. Wavy lines mean wind, or road?"

Bhalon nodded slowly. "I' could well be."

Giselle peered at the stone. "Would the crosses mean death? Or danger? Is it a warning?"

A smile slowly crept across Bhalon's face. "No. I mean, yes; they do mean death, bu' i's no' just a warnin'. I's a rhyme."

"A rhyme?" Samuel asked, incredulously.

"Aye. 'Tis a song, more specifically; a kinfolk children's song." He pointed to the pictures as he recited: "Spring brings th' rains, th' rains, th' rains. Bringer o' death on th' mountain roads. Turn abou', turn abou', turn abou', children, stay safe under the mountain, 'til the sun returns."

"That's uplifting," Giselle said.

"I's meant to serve as a warnin'," Bhalon said. "The mountains are near impassable in the spring; mud would often slide straigh' down th' roads, and carry away anyone foolish enough ta try 'em."

"Why not just teach the children that?"

Bhalon shrugged. "Little 'uns are more like to remember songs than lessons—and this was one o' those lessons ye may only ge' ta test once." He turned back to the stone and hummed to himself as he pressed the corresponding pictures, each of which pressed into the stone before popping back up level with the surface: rain, rain, rain; death, mountain, road; under, mountain, sun.

The party looked around expectantly, but the room remained silent. Grug walked over to the door and pushed, then tried one of the tracked stones. "No move."

Bhalon frowned down at the stone in front of him for a moment, before hesitantly placing his hands to either side and twisting it. The stone, for all of its enormous weight and size, turned smoothly on a central shaft.

Bhalon grunted and began again: rain, rain, rain; death, mountain, road. He paused and grabbed the stone, spinning three times on its axis. Under, mountain, sun. As Bhalon pushed the image of the sun, a loud clunk echoed through the room. Grug and Giselle each moved to one of the boulders near the door and pushed. With a grating of sand and grit, the boulders each slid back toward the wall, settling into place with a thud. Bhalon carefully approached the center of the door and gave it a gentle push. Gliding on nearly-silent hinges and counterweights, the door folded in on itself, splitting into four panels that slid back into the walls on either side of the entrance. Before the party stretched a sloped track, angling downward, with dim blue jewels slowly brightening on either side of the passage. From below came a constant hum of machinery and the sound of metal scraping over stone.

"Well," Bhalon said. "We've got i' open. Let's hope tha' was the hard part."

They were very nearly the last words Bhalon ever uttered. A spinning, circular blade, as broad as Grug was tall, and attached to a long metal arm, dropped from the ceiling at speed, slicing through the space Bhalon had occupied not a breath before, before swooping back up and out of sight again.

"Wha' tha' bloody hell was tha'?" Bhalon said.

Samuel was studying the walls, ceiling, and floor around them. "A near miss perhaps, and certainly a warning. We had best watch our step."

Grug and Giselle both drew their swords, taking the lead, while the rest of the party fell in behind. The floor and walls of the cavern were smooth—unnaturally so. The walls were glassy, as though the stone had been melted, and the floor, though textured and almost sticky, seemed to have been made by compressing small stones and some sort of oil until it had a smooth, uniform surface. The blackness seemed to suck in the light of the jewels on the walls, shimmering like a black river beneath the party's feet. The path sloped gradually downward into the heart of the mountain, following a slow spiral.

At last, they reached the bottom of the spiral, where the black road gave way to polished white stone, and the close walls and ceiling blossomed upward into a large cavern. Soaring ceilings, which must have majestically framed the room in their time, were marred by stalactites stretching down toward the floor, and often meeting their stalagmite counterparts, where they themselves marred the beauty of the otherwise pristine stone floor. Doorways led off of each side of the chamber, though these too had been covered in a few cases by the slow drip of limestone down the cavern's walls.

Samuel turned to Obsidialkin and Emaflintross. "Can you tell which way leads to the jewels?"

The two gnomes moved forward, their eyes unfixed while they focused on following the scent from door to door. When they met at the final door, in the front of the cavern, they chittered excitedly to each other, before returning to share their findings with Shalevelkin.

"Jewels behind every door," the gnarrinshang said. "Even covered ones. Scent strongest from middle door on left. Obsidialkin also smells…" He spoke rapidly with the other gnome for a moment. "Machinery. Iron works, in that direction. Many sounds, many moving parts there, too."

Bhalon grunted. "It migh' be better to try one o' the other ways firs', then. Let's see wha' we're up against before we meet a lot o'them together."

"Agreed," Samuel said. The rest of the party nodded and followed Bhalon to the right side of the room, where they approached the closest door. "Grug, if you would do the honours?"

Grug nodded and carefully pushed down the latching ring on the door, before following with a swift kick. The door banged into the wall behind it, revealing a long hallway with doors on either side. Giselle, assuming that the noise had already given them away to anyone nearby, moved quickly to the first door and pushed it open, her sword held ready. "Nothing," Giselle said. "It looks like these must have been living quarters, but they've been empty for a long time."

Samuel and Grug took turns opening the next couple of doors down the hall, but found nothing but cozy rooms, compact furniture sized for dwarves, and dust. Samuel motioned to the two gnome sniffers: "can you smell anything down here? Is it worth searching the rest of the rooms?"

Emaflintross, who had clearly caught enough of Samuel's words to understand him, chittered to Shalevelkin, who dutifully repeated her words: "nearly halfway down hall, one sapphire, fist-sized, good clarity and cut."

Samuel raised an eyebrow. "You can smell that much about it?"

Shalevelkin translated and Emaflintross grinned and nodded, her gold chains jingling.

"Well then," Sameul said, "let's go. Grug, Giselle, perhaps we should keep checking the doors as we pass them—I would hate to have enemies come up from behind when we're halfway down the corridor."

Grug and Giselle nodded, leading the party through the hall, carefully checking each door, until Emaflintross stopped and chittered at them. She pointed at the next door, identical to all the rest, and nodded.

Grug readied his sword and shoved the door open to reveal yet another apartment, though with one major difference: this one was occupied. Lying half on the bed, and half on the floor, was a vaguely human-shaped body, almost as large as Grug, but made of a silvery metal. Rather than legs, the body had a sphere—or rather, a set of many rings that appeared to fit together precisely into a spherical shape, but capable of reconfiguring themselves at will. Its upper body was a series of metallic limbs and structural braces, through which the party could see the bed beneath, and its face—or rather what they could see of it—had an almost equine shape, with a long muzzle, and a complete absence of anything resembling eyes, ears, or a nose.

Bhalon took the lead, slowly approaching the figure and speaking in a strangely slurred dialect that sounded only vaguely like common, but there was no response. His hand glowing faintly, the dwarf reached out and touched one shoulder, but still there was nothing. "Grug, help me turn it over."

With a groan of metal long unmoved, Grug and Bhalon turned the figure over, the waist swivelling on top of the sphere, rather than turning it. The front of the figure was much the same as the back, with silvery struts defining its shape, but with a blue gem, roughly the size of a gnome's fist, fit into the chest. Bhalon glanced back at Emaflintross and Obsidialkin. "I do no' suppose yer noses can tell ye if i'tis safe ta touch it, can they?"

After a quick discussion with Shalevelkin, the two gnomes shook their heads. "Can smell the gem, and the magic within," the Gnarrinshang said, "but not intent."

Bhalon sighed. "I suppose tha' was too much ta hope for. Move back, Grug. I'll do i'. Mayhap the High Lord will protect me, e'en in my folly." He reached forward, his eyes squinted partially shut, and placed a hand on the gem. The party drew a collective breath, but nothing happened.

"Do you feel anything?" Triwathon asked.

"Nothin'," Bhalon said. "Though it may be tha' it simply isn't strong enough ta work on a dwarf. Let me see if I can get it ou' o'there." He worked his fingers around the edges of the gem's socket until he came to matching divots on either side. He twisted the entire socket counter-clockwise, grinning as the circle of metal around the gem slowly slid back to release its prize. Bhalon held the gem a moment, turning it in his hands, then shrugged. "Still nothin' I can feel. "Any volunteers?"

Giselle hold out her hand, and Bhalon gently placed the gem in it. She closed her eyes, shuddering gently and blew out a slow breath.

"How Giselle feel?" Grug asked.

Giselle flashed a broad grin. "Good. Very good. Like my armour suddenly doesn't weigh anything."

"Ye've grown stronger, then?" Bhalon asked.

"I think so." She walked over to Grug. "Put away your sword for a moment." Once Grug had sheathed his sword, Giselle swept him up into her arms, carrying him with little apparent effort. "Definitely stronger," she said, "though only a bit. I don't think I'm about to go knocking down any walls or throwing boulders." She grinned at Grug. "I kind of like having you where you can't get away, though, barbarian."

Bhalon rolled his eyes. "If you two are quite done, we should probably keep going."

Giselle smiled. "I suppose. You and I can continue this conversation later, Grug." She carefully placed him back on his feet.

"Is that all you can sense down this corridor?" Samuel asked Obsidialkin. The gnome nodded, gesturing that they should go back in the direction they came. "Agreed," Samuel said. Let's keep moving, and see how many smaller gems we can gather."

*　　*　　*

Over the next few hours, the party visited kitchens empty of food, libraries full of scrolls long rotted, living space of every configuration, and even privies. In each, except the privies, they found automatons, not unlike the first, that had either lain down or been struck down where they stood—some in the middle of reading or working in workshops, and others while they moved through rooms. The party returned to the main hall with five gems of various sizes and colours: two of these gave slight increases to strength, now held by Grug and Giselle; another that seemed to make the holder faster and more agile, which Triwathon held; one which Haeronor said made him feel somehow better prepared to cast spells; and one that had no discernable effect at all, but was a very pretty emerald in its own right. Emaflintross held onto it, until they could better determine its use.

Warily, they approached the final door leading from the hall. From behind it came the faint sound of metal scraping against stone, the whirring of enormous motors, and a slight smell of sulphur. "Are we ready?" Samuel asked. They all nodded their agreement, and Grug moved to one of the doors, sword drawn and poised in his other hand.

The scent of sulphur that poured forth from the opened door was not nearly as startling as the heat. It crashed into them in a wave, like emerging from a cold cellar into a sweltering summer's day, making them step back involuntarily. The room was large, though not nearly as large as the great hall, and much less prone to stalactite formation. Instead, it was filled with wide stone columns that whirred as though filled with turbines—which, Samuel realized belatedly, they were. The great turbines were driven by steam, piped in from the floor below, and through each column to make the turbines spin. The steam billowed from the tops of each column toward the ceiling, where a fan pulled it into a series of ducts leading back down through the floor against the side wall.

As the party came into the room, a rusty screech rent the air. Two automatons, very much moving and aware, had emerged from behind one of the columns, their blind faces fixed on the strangers entering their domain. They extended their arms forward, and large blades folded out of their forearms and slid forward to settle into supportive slots in their claw-like hands. Whirring filled the air as the blades, and the hands they were attached to, began to spin, creating a blur of sharpened metal between them and their adversaries. The rings that made up their lower bodies slid over one another in an endlessly-falling motion that propelled them forward at speed.

The party fanned out to give each other room to use their weapons, with Grug and Giselle at the center, and the gnomes tucked in behind them. Triwathon, a thoughtful look on his face, loosed an arrow at the closest automaton's lower half; the arrow caught between two spinning rings, sending the automaton crashing to the ground. It was up again in a moment, the arrow shaft sheared to pieces, and a few of the rings forming a round shield that kept itself aimed at Triwathon. Grug and Giselle moved forward as one, swinging their swords into the whirling mass of steel, in an attempt to shear off hands. Giselle succeeded, her broad blade crashing through one clawed hand, leaving the blade dangling limply from the end of the automaton's ruined wrist. Grug wasn't as lucky, and the whirling blade sent his own bouncing away, leaving a large chip in the edge for good measure. He circled the automaton, blade feinting in again, giving Haeronor an opening to shoot a magic missile into the machine's open back. It exploded just inside the metal skeleton, and the automaton's right arm dropped uselessly, while a number of the circles propelling it forward suddenly stopped spinning, sending the entire metal body lurching toward the floor. Grug swung again, his sword neatly cleaving the metal head from its neck at the same time Bhalon's axe crashed into the its back.

Samuel had moved in to help Giselle with the other automaton, his short blade thrusting up and under the skeletal ribs and in behind the gem socketed in the metal chest. He twisted and pulled, as the automaton shrieked and tried to twist its arms around behind it, but Giselle moved in, grabbing the metal forearm and holding it to keep it from bringing the spinning blade closer to the thief. Samuel's blade finally caught something important within the automaton, and it slumped lifelessly to the floor.

Triwathon gave a low whistle. "How many of those do you suppose are down here?"

Bhalon shrugged. "There's no way ta know. Good idea with th'arrow, by the by."

"Thanks," Triwathon said. "It might have worked, if the rings weren't strong enough to make it through the arrow shaft. Haeronor, could you do something to my arrows to make them harder, without making them heavier?"

The mage looked thoughtful for a moment. "No. I can make them harder, but not without increasing their weight."

"Do what you can. It may decrease my range a bit, but the trade may be worth it."

Haeronor took half a dozen of Triwathon's arrows in his hands, and began speaking under his breath. Golden light washed over the arrows for a moment, then receded, leaving each arrow with a slight sheen. He handed them back to the ranger. "That's the best I can do."

Triwathon hefted on of the arrows in his hand and nodded. "Not bad at all. I can make that work."

Obsidialkin and Emaflintross were already busy extracting the gems from the chest of each automaton, ghoulish grins on their faces as they pried and hacked the metal chests apart. They stood back up and chittered excitedly to Shalevelkin. "Gems make everything clearer. Stronger scents, better vision, better hearing," the Gnarrinshang told the party. "Can almost taste the gems below—and there are many." The two gemsniffers grinned, slipping the gems into their pockets and cautiously leading the way to the mouth of a side passage. Just enough light filtered in past the shadow of the doorway to show the floor descending gently as it curved off toward their right.

Grug and Giselle moved into the lead again, their swords held ready for thrusting rather than broad swings in the confined space. The air was cooler than it had been in the central room, but the stooped ceiling made it feel even more suffocating, and the moving shadows of Haeronor's mage light playing off of the natural dips in the stone made every muscle in Grug's chest and arms twitch, as he constantly shifted his grip to ready for foes hiding in every ghostly silhouette.

The minutes crawled by, and the heat slowly increased. Sweat beaded on Grug's face, dripping off of him periodically to splash silently onto the stone floor. As they came around a corner, an even greater blast of heat dried the sweat on his skin momentarily, the air shimmering and shifting in front of his eyes, distorting the cavern before them. A dozen stone tubes, twice his height or more, gushed steam from their tops and radiated a heat so intense that Grug was amazed the rock itself didn't boil. Heavy structural arms, anchored in the stone floor, provided pivots to allow the tubes to pour, though what giants could do such a thing, Grug couldn't imagine. Broad stone tables rose from the floor, evenly spaced between the tubes, some with what looked almost like clay bathing tubs sitting atop them.

Bhalon pushed past Grug and Giselle, staring in wonder. "A

foundry? Here? An' runnin' on the ground's own heat? I did no' think i' twas possible."

Triwathon surveyed the room. "And running, after all this time? How could that be?"

Bhalon looked thoughtful. "Well, with no fires ta tend, I suppose—"

Bhalon's words were cut off as Emaflintross hurtled into him, throwing them both the ground in time to avoid a fireball that seared through the air where Bhalon's face had been. "Tharmakhul!" the dwarf thundered, lurching back to his feet and raising his mace before him, as an automaton stomped forth from the far end of the room.

Standing taller than the stone tubes, and made from a golden metal blued and discoloured from heat, the automaton had a head the size and shape of a boulder, and legs large enough to crush Grug underfoot while standing. It stared dispassionately at them, it's arm still pointing toward them and glowing yellow from the fireball it had just sent toward them.

An arrow sprang past Grug's shoulder toward the automaton, as Triwathon attempted to pierce one of the metallic eyes, but it ricocheted off of the giant's cheek, as did the magic missile that followed it. Fire sprang from the automaton's hand again and the party threw themselves to either side. Grug rolled to his feet just as the ground beneath him began to heave; the automaton had clearly decided to close the distance, and each of its heavy footfalls shook the bedrock beneath them. Grug came to his feet again, his legs coiled to start sprinting, but he had nowhere to go. The tubes sat too close to the walls to allow him to flank the giant figure; the heat would cook him as he ran. Running back to the cave would only leave his friends alone to face the beast; and there was no way to move through the centre of the gallery without being directly in the automaton's path—surely a suicide mission. Grug sprang straight toward the automaton, bellowing a war cry that was echoed by Giselle, already running at his side.

The churning iron legs stomped toward them like the sounding of giant war drums. It was all Grug could do to stay on his feet and keep running as the ground shook beneath him. With no more than a dozen monstrous strides between them, the automaton suddenly shrank, the entire imposing height evaporating, to bring his head only a few feet above Grug's own. Grug and Giselle skidded to a stop, and it took Grug a few moments to realize that it wasn't so much that the automaton had shrunk, as it was that its legs had disappeared into the stone beneath it. Silent but for the screeching of metal against stone, the monster raised its arm again to fire.

There was a loud clang, as a stone soared through the air, flying unerringly from Shalevelkin's hand to lodge itself in the barrel of the automaton's wrist.

Unperturbed or unaware, the monster aimed for Grug and Giselle and fired.

The explosion shook the room. Grug turned his face away, but there was no way to cover his torso and legs from the dozens of tiny shards of molten metal flying through the air in his direction. Giselle yelped and cursed beside him.

When Grug's vision had returned, he looked carefully back at the automaton, rooted in the floor like a lightning-blasted tree. The explosion had shattered its entire arm, and a good portion of its chest and face on the left side, but the giant's right eye still stared at them, while it's arm heaved against the ground, trying to push itself free of the stone. Shalevelkin walked up next to Grug and Giselle, his eyes open wide in wonder at the automaton. "Apologies," he said. "Stone beneath too…dense. Could not send down farther."

Giselle shook her head gently, her eyes never leaving the automaton. "You owe us no apology, Gnarrinshang. You likely just saved our lives. Thank you."

Bhalon and the rest of the party joined them, just out of the monster's reach. "Wha' the bloody hell do we do now?" the dwarf demanded. "We canno' go around the smelters, and this great heap can reach us if we go up the centre."

Before anyone could come up with a suggestion, a voice boomed through the room, loud and deep enough to shake the solid walls of the cavern. Bhalon's eyes opened wide in surprise, then narrowed as he concentrated on the words, which sounded to Grug like gibberish. After a moment, Bhalon bellowed something back in dwarfish, and the automaton before them slumped, falling as far forward as its sunken lower half would allow.

"We ha' been invited in," Bhalon said shortly, his face tense.

"By whom?" Giselle asked.

"I do no' know. Bu' i' speaks Dwemer, and seems ta understand my Dwarvish well enough."

"Well, I suppose it's only polite to go and introduce ourselves," Haeronor said, walking carelessly past the now-silent automaton, and toward the back wall of the cavern. The rest of the party followed cautiously, watching for any signs of a trap. As Haeronor neared the wall, it slid open, folding back on itself like the front door to the ruin and sliding silently into the adjacent wall. A moment after the party had all made their way through the opening, it swung closed. Though it closed just as quietly as it opened, Grug couldn't help but imagine the panels crashing closed like the heavy, stone doors of a tomb.

Beyond the opening, the passageway was again lit by soft, blue lamps. This time, however, the passage was short enough for them to make out the glow of the next room, a bright, powerful, and multi-hued radiance that danced on the dark stone walls, consuming the softer light, more than blending with it. The source was not only obvious to the party, but aggressively so, the moment they stepped into the room; in the middle, on a pile of crushed and ancient pallets, lay an automaton that made the giant from the smelting room seem small and dull. Languishing in what seemed a deliberate pose of ease, the enormous figure shone with light from dozens, if not hundreds, of gems of all shapes and sizes, each pulsing with its own inner light. Diamonds, sapphires, rubies, amethysts, and emeralds of every shape, size, and cut, studded limbs, torso, and head, shimmering enticingly. Even the automaton's eyes were gems, sapphires the size of Grug's fist. The eyes were fixed on the party as they entered the room, weapons still at the ready.

Twin groans rose from Obsidialkin and Emaflintross and they staggered, falling to their knees.

"Wha' t'is it?" Bhalon asked, trying to keep one eye on the giant before them. "Are ye under attack somehow?"

Emaflintross shook her head, then stared imploringly at Shakevelkin, muttering something in heavily-slurred words.

The Gnarrinshang looked at Bhalon. "It is that there are too many gems. Senses overwhelmed."

Bhalon nodded, squeezing Obsidialkin's shoulder as he strode up to stand next to Grug, Giselle, and Haeronor. They stared at the automaton, waiting for it to speak.

It appeared that the automaton had been waiting for Bhalon, as well. "Durath ginnen ithca, stalduc," it intoned, its voice shaking the ground beneath their feet.

Bhalon nodded his head gravely, "Eshkae duroc nedal blathro, stalduc. Ishma dodoth nigta?"

The automaton stared for a moment at Bhalon, unblinking—which was somewhat unsurprising for a being with gems for eyes. "Yes," it boomed at last. "I have some common tongue."

"We thank ye'," Bhalon said. "I understand ye well enough in Dwemer, but m'friends do no'. I' twould be impolite."

The automaton's eyes glimmered, a deeper blue welling up within the sapphires for a moment. "I do so *hate* to be impolite," it said sarcastically. "Especially to a band of thieves, intent on robbing and pillaging the remains of a civilization greater than their own."

Bhalon licked his lips nervously, while Grug and Giselle shifted their grips on their weapons. "Our apologies, o' course," Bhalon offered. "We did no' know tha' there were any…Dwemer…left."

"Ah, so you came to clean the carcass, and found that the corpse could still kick."

Bhalon awkwardly rubbed the back of his neck. "Somethin' like tha', yeah." He paused for a moment, ordering his thoughts. "We would no' have come a'tall, bu' for greatest need. A sorcerer walks the land, intent on—"

"Yes, yes," the automaton rumbled. "No doubt there's some world-saving reason you need the fruits of my people's labours, and you feel entitled to take them. I care not for your needs, or your people, *cousin*." He scowled contemptuously at them all. "You are lesser creatures, of lesser races. I would spit on all of you…if I had any spit." He sagged back onto his pallets.

Grug's brows furrowed in concentration. "If Dwemer better, why gone?"

"Because even the greatest of us make mistakes." He seemed to choke back a sob. "We could have been gods!" he bellowed. The party dropped to their knees, hands over their ears. "We were, for a while."

"Hubris," Bhalon muttered. "Only the High Lord can make a god."

"What would you know of it?" the automaton demanded shrilly. "What would you call a race that never died? A race that conquered time itself? A race that could make itself as intelligent, as strong, or as agile as it needed to be? They would be gods!"

Giselle's eyes widened. "Those machines in the rest of the ruins…they weren't just machines, were they?"

The automaton stared at her. "No," he said finally. "Those were my kin."

Bhalon looked disgusted. "Bu' how? Why?"

The automaton sighed. "Did you know gems could hold souls, little cousin?" Not just the fragments of magic that we put into them to run our machines, but entire souls? We thought it was an accident, at first, a process gone terribly wrong—but it only ever happened on occasion, and only when we tried to make powerful gems. We were shocked and horrified, at first, to find that those who died imbuing the gems were trapped within them. Then we realized what a gift we had found."

"Blasphemy," Bhalon growled.

"Perhaps." The automaton shrugged, with a screeching of metal. "What did we care for such foolish, religious distinctions? We had found a way to live forever. One had only to have a body in which to put their soul gem, and we had more bodies than we knew what to do with-- bodies that defied age and could be upgraded to meet our every need. We perfected the process, and within a year, there was not a Dwemer left in their original flesh."

"But of all of them, you're the only one we found alive—unless those guards outside…" Giselle said.

"No. Those are but machines. We…overreached. We should have moved slower, tested longer. We didn't realize that the size of a gem, the clarity, the flaws—all of it affected how well it could hold a soul. The first began to lose their vitality within a decade. By the time we realized the cause, and the solution for it, more than half of the Dwemer were already gone."

"Then where are the others?" Haeronor asked. "Can we meet them?"

The automaton scowled. "You just have. I am the Dwemer, fool."

Bhalon stared, his eyes roving at the shimmer gems studded all over the massive, metallic form. "Why are they no' in their own bodies?"

"At first, we weren't sure if they could stay there safely. The only way to keep the smaller gems energized was to keep them near greater ones. It also took us quite some time to figure out how to move a soul back out of one gem and into another, without losing the soul entirely. By the time we'd figured all of that out, well…it was hard for me to part company with any of them."

Giselle's face wrinkled in disgust. "And so you've kept them prisoner with you?"

"Prisoners?" the automaton scoffed. "They are part of something greater, now! A Dwemer god!"

"Some god," Triwathon drawled. "Sitting alone in a ruin, miles underground."

The automaton smiled wickedly. "Indeed, elf. Surely, I should be in the world above; the Dwemer should be rulers, should they not? And yet here I am, in a body made to endure, but not to move. Whatever shall I do? If only there were some foolish mortals that could carry me with them to the surface."

Grug grunted. "Too big. Too heavy."

The automaton did its best to roll its jeweled eyes. "Not literally, fool. I need only a vessel to carry a soul, to pave the way for a Dwemer return."

"Need big jar?"

The automaton looked over at Bhalon. "He's a bright one, isn't he? That's helpful, actually. The dumber ones don't tend to fight back as much."

"Ye'll no' touch 'im." Bhalon growled, raising his mace.

With a clanking and screeching, the dark edges of the room came to life, dozens of smaller automatons rising from the shadows and surrounding the party.

"Don't worry, cousin. Once I'm done with the barbarian, I have plenty more souls for the rest of you." The great sapphire eyes turned back to Grug. "Now, where were we?"

Darkness washed over Grug's eyes, and he felt as though every fibre of his body was being torn away individually. He could hear Giselle's outraged scream and Bhalon's roar, but they were muffled, distant. For a moment he could hear the automaton's voice in his head, imploring him to let go, to stop resisting, and then he was once again adrift in a void, the darkness slithering over his skin, blinding and encompassing him, sliding into his nose, throat, and ears.

From within the ether came the voices of the gods.

"An eighteen saving roll? That's ridiculous, Russell! You know it's only a d20, right?"

"Stop whining and roll."

"But it's not fair! Why is it always my character you do this sort of thing to, and why does the saving roll need to be so high?"

"Because the automaton is over a thousand years old, has half a race's souls inside of it, and its willpower is off the charts. And it always happens to your character because you decided to spend all of his points in strength and fortitude, and there weren't enough left for decent intelligence and willpower. Now make the damned roll."

Grug heard the clatter of a single dice, followed by what was clearly swearing, though he didn't recognize the words.

"Ha ha! Suck it, Russell! A 20! You have to roll to check for epic failure."

"Fine," the other god replied. The dice clattered again. "Oh, hell."

"A one?" the god shrieked. "A one??? When you had the power of all of the automaton's souls being used to try to take over Grug, and you epically failed? Let's see it, then."

With a rush and a shock as though falling from a great height, Grug slammed home into his body once more just in time to see the automaton clamp his hands over the sides of his head. The room shook with the unearthly screams of hundreds of souls being torn apart, as the automaton's massive fingers tore into its metal skull, shearing away the golden skin to reveal the largest diamond Grug had even seen, pulsing with blinding flickers of light. The faceless automaton screamed again, steam boiling up through pipes in the back of the monster's throat that were now exposed. Then the mighty fingers closed upon the diamond, straining, clenching, as the screams grew shriller and more agonized.

With a crack, the diamond split, a flaw too small to see with the naked eye providing a pathway for the gem to rive. At once, the brilliant lights within it dimmed and faded to darkness. All around the party, automatons clattered to the floor with the sound of a thousand pots and pans thrown down a set of stairs. The party stared at one another, and at the field of metallic carnage around them in disbelief.

"Wha' tha bloody 'ell was tha'?" Bhalon demanded.

Grug felt himself blushing. "Giant tried to take Grug's mind. Gods said no."

Triwathon giggled, and then started to laugh so hard that tears ran down his cheeks. When he could finally catch a gasping breath, he asked "are you telling me that you're so dumb that trying to take over your brain broke his?"

"Triwathon!" Bhalon said. "Mind yer tongue!"

Grug shrugged. "Gods said 'epic failure'."

Bhalon looked confused. "Well, I do no' know wha' tha' means, but well done, none-the-less, lad. Wha'e'er i'twas ye did."

"So what do we do now?" Haeronor asked.

"We get word back to the guild," Samuel said, looking at the massive pile of gems on and around the automaton. "We're going to need help getting all of this out of here."

CHAPTER 9

HOW TO TELL YOUR GEM FROM A HOLE IN THE GROUND

Samuel felt the air rush into his lungs, as though he had just come up after swimming a long distance underwater. His eyes opened on the wooden council table he had seen so many times before, this time encircled by guildmasters or their proxies from across the continent.

"Cooper?" Donnal, the guildmaster from Morath, the capital city of Adana, asked. "Are you alright?"

Samuel blinked, trying to read the faces around the room and get some sense of what was going on.

Yes, thank you. Where were we?"

Donnal shrugged. "I don't want to speak for the group, but I think we were about to yell 'yeah!'"

Samuel stared blankly. "What?"

"Well, you told us about the sorcerer and his plans, and asked if we would join you. We were, again, not wanting to speak for the whole group here, about to yell 'yeah!' Then you sort of went glassy eyed for a moment."

"Oh." Samuel looked around the table again, where many were

nodding in agreement. "Just like that?"

Swift Eddie, guildmaster of a small city called Hope, in Varasta, grinned crookedly. "What do you think we are? Politicians? Clearly there's danger to us all here, and a way to remedy it. As guildmasters, we have the power to act in times of immediate threat without consulting our boards. What's the point of power, if you're not going to use it?"

There were nods around the table.

Donnal smiled. "So, guildmaster, why not just ask if we're with you, and we can go from there?"

"Okay," Samuel said tentatively. "Are you with me?"

Yeahs were yelled and the table was pounded.

"Good," Donnal said. "Now that that's settled, let's get some lunch."

*　　*　　*

With so many gems to sort from the caves of the Dwemer, Emaflintross and Obsidialkin were soon overwhelmed. The scents and flavours of each meshed with those around them, leaving the two gnomes giddy and exhausted with only a fraction of the stones sorted.

Samuel chaffed at the delay. Each minute that ticked by brought the final battle closer; spies had already brought word of the sorcerer's troops arriving and garrisoning the castle at Cawda, a massive border fortress where Belakeer and Varasta met. Samuel would have been happy to let them sit there and rot, while assassins slowly decimated their patrols, but every day brought more troops from across the continent—and with them, an expected increase in the sorcerer's power, as he drew on the very life forces of those that joined him. It was impossible to know where the tipping point was, when the sorcerer would have enough people to draw upon, enough raw power to put his plan into action. The only certain thing was that there would be no going back.

"Someone is going to start aiming at you through that window, if you keep staring out of it," Triwathon said.

Samuel startled out of his reverie, his eyes again focusing on the sight of the sun rising over Shimano. Triwathon, his eyes still on the guildmaster, shoveled another forkful of eggs into his mouth. Apparently satisfied with his third helping, he pushed his plate away and took a long swallow from the tankard beside it. "You should eat. The armies won't arrive any faster if you starve yourself."

Samuel tried to remember if he had ever heard the ranger string so many words together before, but his mind wasn't focused enough. He sat down at the board table with a sigh, pulling a pastry toward him. "It's not the armies, Triwathon—though if you've any ideas on how to get them closer, faster, and without tipping our hand to the sorcerer, I'd certainly hear them. It's the gems. They're powerful enough that our sniffers are overwhelmed to be on the same side of the city, much less sorting through them all day. After testing a handful of them, they get giddy and have to spend the rest of the day resting in a cave somewhere. At this rate, the armies could stop for a feast and ballroom dancing lessons and still make it here before we know what aid we can give them."

Triwathon shrugged. "Then give them out randomly."

Samuel laughed. "That would be chaos. The enormously strong breaking their bows while those perceptive enough to put an arrow through a keyhole struggle to wield maces without hitting those on horseback, who would be agile enough to jump over the front lines if they were on foot. It would be insanity."

"Hmm…" Triwathon tipped his chair back as he thought things through. "So four or five of us take turns trying gems—"

"Won't work," Samuel sighed exasperatedly. "Switching between them is exhausting. I tried and got through even fewer than Emaflintross or Obsidialkin could in a sitting—and it's not easy to determine, with some of the lesser gems, what they're really doing. You almost need standard tests."

"So, you need a whole bunch of people and some tests, right?"

"Yes."

"How many thieves do you have in the city right now?" Triwathon asked with a sly smile.

Samuel stared at him for a moment, feeling a smile of his own growing across his face. "A bunch."

"I thought you might."

"And I bet our gnomish friends might help us devise some tests."

Triwathon nodded. "I would guess so."

"And perhaps some trusted few, with more powerful gems, might dissuade any thieves from, well…thieving."

"You might even wish to have Obsidialkin and Emaflintross just hold back the strongest gems for their own review and leave the more minor ones to the thieves. Just a thought."

Samuel grinned, feeling better than he had in days. "Pass the eggs, would you? We've got a long day ahead."

*   *   *

Samuel had thought that by the third time he had seen a youth from the pickpockets pick up a rock three times their size and throw it, if would have lost its excitement and surprise; this was not the case.

Oler, a blond-haired, 10-year-old pickpocket, with a face so disarmingly plain that he seemed to pass through any crowd unnoticed, smiled, his eyes twinkling mischievously. "Well, now. That's a bit of alright, innit?"

Samuel couldn't help but smile. "You're not wrong, Oler. That one's clearly a strength gem. Looks to be middling strength. Put it in the pile beside Marcus."

Oler batted his eyelashes innocently. "Couldn't I just—"

"No," Marcus said flatly. "You couldn't. Give me that stone, or you'll fly a lot farther than that rock just did."

Oler made a face at Marcus, but did as he was told before making his way to the other side of the room and out the door.

"Next!" Samuel called.

Another pickpocket entered, his curly brown locks pointing in every direction. "Hello, Guildmaster."

"Hello, Jamis. Please take a gem from the table next to the door and come over to the middle of the room."

Jamis did as he was told, presenting himself before Samuel and

106

Nathanial.

"Put the gem in your shirt. Make sure it's touching your skin. Then try to pick up that stone."

"Guild master?"

"Don't worry about how big it is. That gem should be giving you some sort of power; we need to figure out which one."

"Yes, sir." Jamis put the gem inside of his shirt, bent down and strained at the boulder for a moment before shaking his head. "I can't lift it."

"No problem," Samuel replied. Pick up three little stones from the pile in front of me, and try to throw them through those three hoops, spaced toward the front of the room."

Again, Jamis did as he was told, but it was clear from the first stone that the boy had no special assistance with his aim.

"Hmm," Samuel said. "Not perception either, then. Marcus, test his constitution."

Marcus walked over and smacked Janis across the back of the head.

"Oww! What did you do that for, Marcus?"

Samuel frowned. "Not constitution, and probably not agility, either, or he'd have made a better show of getting out of the way. Janis, do you have a coin on you?"

"Why?" Janis demanded. "Are you going to rob me, as well as beat me?"

Samuel smiled sympathetically. "Sorry, Janis. It's just the tests we need to go through. Nothing personal. Now, do you have a coin?"

"Yes," Janis replied sulkily.

"Good. I want you to flip it ten times in a row, showing Marcus each time. If it comes up heads less than 5 times, Marcus gets to hit you some more."

"*What?*"

Nathanial frowned at his son. "Now, Samuel—"

"Just let the tests do what they're supposed to, father. Go ahead, Jamis."

Jamis glanced nervously at Marcus and began flipping the coin. "Heads. Heads. Heads. Heads. Heads. Do I keep going?"

"Finish it off," Samuel said.

"Heads. Heads. Heads. Tails. Heads."

Samuel smiled warmly. "How lucky for you." Put the gem in the small pile in front of me, please Janis. Then you may go."

Janis did as he was told, nervously hedging around Marcus on his way out of the room.

Samuel made a note in the ledger next to him. "Well, that's the last one. Luck—and decently strong, I suspect, though it's hard to tell with the lucky ones. It could just be dumb luck." He stood up and stretched. "Marcus, would you please lock these ones up with the rest? We'll need to—"

The door swung open with a crash, and a pimply 15 year-old ran in, his voice cracking. "Guildmaster! Guildmaster!"

"What is it, Wilf? What's the matter?"

"There's been a courier, Guildmaster! From the dwarves! They're in eastern and northern Varasta already, and converging on Cawda. They'll be there in less than a week!"

Nathanial sighed loudly. "With the orcs already at the border of Southern Haeraxa, as well. We may have finished just in time, son. Like it or not, we will soon see the start of a war."

Samuel nodded slowly. So much time had been spent preparing, spying on the sorcerer, organizing the thieves, finding and sorting the gems. But it all came down to this. "Marcus, ready the guilds. Let's go get the bastard."

CHAPTER 10

IT'S THE FINAL COUNTDOWN (BAH NAH NAT NAH)

The lines were intricate. Every symbol needed to be perfect—and there was still no guarantee that the portal would work. Darathan had plundered every library he had come across and tortured information from every conjurer he could find just to get this far, and he was still combining spells and figures in a way that had never been contemplated before.

The amulet sat cold and uncomfortable around his neck, the sharp angles scraping his flesh as he moved, but his brain whirred and spun with flashes of insight he never would have possessed without it; he could see the flaws in the lines that he had planned before stealing the amulet and correct them instinctively, like a master painter correcting an apprentice's work. He was nearing the end of the design, and the carefully-constructed swirls and symbols took up half of the dungeon floor.

The power he needed was nearly collected, as well. Darathan could feel it, pushing at the edge of his senses as he gently set crystals of salt, sulphur, and ash into place. Each country's citizens that swore their fealty was like a light at the edge of his consciousness, a beacon of power to drink from. The soldiers in the castle bloomed even brighter in his awareness, like a wellspring that he could drink deeply from. Even now, he might have enough, if he drained some of them completely, but soldiers had uses beyond feeding his magic; his scouts warned that the armies they had been tracking would arrive any day now.

A horn rang out from the walls, startling Darathan momentarily. His hand shook and a few salt crystals fell from his palm. Stopping himself short of a gasp, the sorcerer refocused his energies and, ever so gently, pushed the crystals that had fallen improperly back into line. Only when he was sure that they were perfectly aligned, with no strays, did he stand up and place the remaining salt in his palm back into one of the bags hanging from his belt.

A sharp clattering on the stairs prefaced a gentle knock on the dungeon door.

"Come."

The door opened to admit a tall red-haired man in plate armour. Any good looks the man might have had were spoiled by an ugly scar across his brow and face, and a patch over his left eye.

"Lanner, why is it that commanders always seem to be missing an eye?" Darathan mused aloud. "Is it such a common injury that a man is bound to receive it by the time he rises to command, or is it part of the selection process?"

Lanner, the mercenary commander that Darathan had hired to help him weld together his Belekeeran, Varastan, and Adanan forces, had become used to these little tangents from his employer. He shrugged. "Perks of leadership, I suppose, Your Majesty."

"Hmm. And what news have you come to share? Have the last of the Varastans finally joined us?"

"Umm…No, Majesty. I'm afraid not."

The sorcerer arched an eyebrow. "Then it has begun?"

"Yes, Majesty. The main force is nearly here—humans, orcs, and dwarves. No sign of the gnomes that our scouts can see, nor the barbarians."

"No matter. Soon enough, the portal will be finished, and their numbers will be irrelevant. Do you have the trinket I gave you?"

Lanner put a hand involuntarily over a satchel tied to his belt. "I do."

"Good. I trust you will know when best to use it. Do not fail me."

"Of course, Your Majesty."

"Now get out. Hold them off. Do whatever you must, but keep them out of the walls long enough for me to finish."

Lanner bowed and sidled from the room, closing the door softly behind him, but Darathan was already too preoccupied to notice, his hand reaching into his right belt pouch for more powdered sulphur.

*　　*　　*

Samuel awoke standing in the middle of a field, surrounded by armed and armoured thieves. "Oh, hell."

Marcus' head swivelled back and forth, trying to spot the danger. "What is it, Guildmaster?"

"Nothing, Marcus. Just…nothing." Samuel quickly scanned through the events that he seemed to remember leading up to this point: the dwarvish and orcish armies had been assembling near Cawda; the thieves guilds from across the continent had mobilized; the gnomes had brought in a special team, but he couldn't quite remember where, or if he'd been told; and, following Haeronor's near-miraculous change of heart toward other races, a contingent of elvish wizards had joined the fray.

"Where's Grug?"

"I'm here, Samuel," Grug's deep voice said from over the guildmaster's right shoulder. He caught Samuel's eyes. "I just arrived, too."

"Good. Do you know where the rest are?"

Grug thought for a moment. "Yes. They're with their own forces: Triwathon has hand-picked the best archers from all the races, Bhalon is leading the dwarves, Giselle is trying to hold the orcish clans together, and Haeronor is with his order. They have all given the gems you assigned out as best they see fit."

Samuel noted the deep blue jewel swinging on a short chain from

Grug's neck. "And you, Grug? Are you sure you don't want to change that for another gem? With your strength already…"

"No. I'd rather have my wits about me. I don't think I'll be planning any strategies with this one, but at least I don't have to ask what everyone means all the time."

"Fair enough, my friend."

A messenger came bounding across the field, like a gazelle in full flight, and nearly as fast. "Guildmaster, the orcs and the dwarves are ready."

"Thank you. And the special unit?"

"Formed up and ready to go."

"Perfect. Tell them to prepare to advance, on my signal."

The messenger bounded away again.

"Special unit?" Grug asked.

Samuel grinned. "Orcs with heavy armour, shields, and gems of constitution, surrounding dwarves with a battering ram. The orcs provide the cover to get to the gates, and then the dwarves break through them. Too bad we couldn't give the dwarves gems of constitution, as well; they'd basically be unkillable, I think."

Grug laughed. "Probably. Why not just have the mages blast through the gates, though?"

"Haeronor says they would have to get too close. We could armour them, and give them gems of constitution, but he said they would do better work unarmoured, and with gems of intelligence."

"Makes sense."

"He also thinks that the sorcerer is going to have something prepared, something we will need the mages for."

Grug sighed. "He's probably right on that, too. The sorcerer should have more than enough power to keep a few spells going at this point, especially if they're prepared in advance."

They stood silently for a few minutes, as they waited for the messenger to make it across their entire line. Finally, a small puff of red smoke from the mages told them that everyone was ready.

"Marcus," Samuel said. "Raise the banner. Let's rip the demon-lover apart."

CHAPTER 11

BALLROOM BLITZKRIEG

Grug's heart pounded in his chest, and he dearly wished that he had opted for a gem of constitution, just in case. He had seen many battles (he thought), but the sheer chaos of what was unfolding before him was otherworldly, and the realization that even a stray hit from an ally could be enough to cripple him, was unnerving. After all, it was one thing to know that your allies have gems of strength, and another thing entirely to watch an orc rip a fully-grown tree out of the ground and throw it at a castle wall.

Thieves shot past Grug in every direction, all moving with the speed and grace of birds in flight to avoid arrows, while launching their own stones and arrows up at the walls with bows and slings. Beside them, the orcs charged, ladders in hand. Despite their strength and heavy armour, the arrows were taking a toll, and those at the front had begun throwing not only trees, but rocks the size of heads at the archers on the walls. Beyond them, Grug knew the special unit of orcs and dwarves would be hanging back, waiting for the archers atop the walls to be sufficiently distracted before they pushed onward toward the gate.

All told, things seemed to be going according to plan. Grug knew the moment that the thought ran through his head that he was asking the universe for trouble—and it delivered.

A man in gilded plate armour appeared at the top of the wall. Leaning back, he threw an object forward, into the middle of the orcish ranks, before disappearing again. For a moment, nothing happened. Then, from beneath the feet of the orcs, a blackness began to spread and grow. When it was horse-sized, its neck began to stretch, and its wings to expand, while its body ballooned from horse-sized to house-sized and beyond.

Orcs and dwarves began to scream and fall back as the black dragon roared its displeasure at the host around it and plowed into those nearest its legs, its massive wings scything through the ranks as it spun and bit, crushing bone and armour with equal ease in its jaws.

Grug had a moment of panic at the thought that Giselle might be one of the orcs being trampled or masticated. The Nalragga had chosen a gem of constitution—and a powerful one—rather than the gems of strength that most of the elite orcs chose, so that she would be more likely to resist injury and remain in command longer, but it was hard to imagine anything that might stand up to the spectacular force of a black dragon.

* * *

Giselle looked down the throat of a dragon, and saw her doom boiling forth; liquid flames erupting from the belly of the beast, churning and sloshing their way up its throat to burst forth as searing flames from its mouth. There was no escape, no dodging, only the certainty of death come calling for her and Druskar, who stood, as ever, at her shoulder.

The dragon appeared easily as surprised as Giselle when certain death failed to take place. The flames crashed into an invisible shield that wrapped around the dragon's mouth, forcing the flames back next to its jaws an up past its horns in a plume that shot fifteen feet into the air. Bellowing in rage, the dragon tried again, but succeeded only in burning the sky above him.

As the dragon's roar faded away into confusion, Giselle could hear a deep, resonant chanting emerge from behind the orcs, as the Tree and

Leaf Order began shaping another spell of their own. Haeronor stood at their forefront, intense concentration written upon his face as he struggled to keep the shield in place despite the dragon's efforts. Above the elves, the light itself seemed to coalesce, the rays of sun to bend and shape themselves into a form as big as the black dragon before it. Chimes jangled discordantly in the air, like a crystal chandelier swinging in a gale, as the diamond dragon launched itself downward like a spear toward its foe. Druskar barely managed to swing Giselle back and out of the way before the two dragons slammed together, biting and tearing at one another as they rolled toward the castle wall.

"Ogrimm's teeth," Druskar bellowed. "What in the nine hells have we gotten ourselves into?"

Before Giselle could answer, a gruff, grating voice rang out: "Watch the profanity, boy. We've barely started the fun part!" Mordeth charged past the both of them, grabbing hold of the end of a siege ladder and hoisting it onto his shoulder.

"You heard the priest," Giselle bellowed. "To the ladders! Leave the dragons space, but get your orcish backsides up those walls before I make priests of all of you!"

*　*　*

With unceasing booms that shook even the ground beneath them, the dwarves slammed home the battering ram into the center of the castle gates. All around them, in full armour, and carrying massive tower shields, their orcish guard absorbed punishment. Arrows stuck from every joint in every suit of armour, but the steel was thick and their skin might as well have been hardened leather itself. Stones, thrown from the walls above, skipped off of helms, denting them, but hardly fazing the warriors wearing them. Bhalon stood at the forefront of the dwarves, heaving with all his might with every swing of the ram, his lips moving constantly in silent prayer. The head of the ram glowed silver, and the sharp sounds of cracking wood began to ring out with each hit.

"Heave!" Svellin called from across the ram, and a chunk of the gate flew into the courtyard. "Heave!" Another crack, and the gate began to cave. "Here it is, boys! HEAVE!"

The timbers wedging the gate in place shattered, and the doors flew inward, knocking half a dozen soldiers back into their next line. With a clattering of armour, they all fell to the ground, as bowstrings twanged and a flurry of arrows rained down into the lines of the orcs and dwarves. A low horn blew and a line of cavalry erupted from inner courtyard, charging toward the dwarvish lines.

Bhalon drew back his silver hammer, glimmering with righteous rage, and flung it toward the oncoming horses before pulling his mace from his belt. "Come on lads! For tha High Lord!"

*   *   *

The booming from above had largely stopped, which likely meant that the gate had been battered down. No matter. They were too late. Chanting, Darathan took careful, intricate steps through the design he had wrought, weaving through a dance as important as the words he spoke. With each footfall, another part of the design solidified, etching itself deep in the stone floor. Sweat rolled down the sorcerer's cheek, and he carefully wiped it away on his sleeve without breaking the rhythm of his movements. He would not fail. He would confront the gods, and take the power from them for his own—and no pathetic army of misfits was going to stop him.

CHAPTER 12

SHOWDOWN

By the time Grug made it into the courtyard, it had devolved into chaos. Dwarves and orcs, alone, or in groups of two or three, tore through the ranks of terrified soldiers, often throwing the soldiers (and sometimes their horses) back at their own lines. The air was full of screaming, smoke from the inevitable fire, and the smell of death. Still, it was better than being chewed on by a dragon, Grug supposed.

Spotting Samuel's group of elite thieves on the east side of the courtyard, Grug began to bull his way through the melee, his axe carving a path through the soldiers. As he got closer, he watched in awe as the guildmaster seemed to flow through his enemies, his sword and dagger dealing out death in equal measure as his opponents struggled to close the distance to him. He stabbed, parried, and moved with unearthly swiftness, his face intent but calm.

"Samuel!"

Samuel dispatched the last enemy near him and nodded to the barbarian. "Grug. How goes the fight?"

"It looks well. The dragon the mages summoned seems to have held off the black dragon, and we're doing well enough here. Surely, the sorcerer's power must be waning with so many dead on his side."

"Don't bet on it," Grug replied. "I expect he's pulling power from every death, as well. We need to find him. Now."

Samuel nodded. "He must be inside the main keep, but we haven't had time to breach it, yet. There's still too many soldiers. Shalevelkin said he was going to take his gnomes through the stone and try to open up the keep from the inside, but I haven't seen any of them yet."

Grug looked around what he could see of the east courtyard, which was still full of clusters of thieves and orcs fighting the sorcerer's heavily-armed Adanan and Belakeeran troops. "Where are the Varastans? I thought he had Varasta under his control, as well."

"I don't know. Mind you, we were supposed to have your people coming down from Narran by now, too, and we haven't seen them. It's possible the two met along the way and the survivors haven't made it here yet. I don't think we can count on them coming now, anyway."

Grug nodded. "Alright. Let's make our way to the entrance of the inner keep, if we can, and try to bludgeon our way in as we wait for the gnomes."

"Agreed. Marcus! We've got to get to the keep entrance!"

The big man nodded, motioning them to follow before he began cutting his way through Belakeeran troops with ease. Though not as slick as Samuel, Marcus' every move was precise and calculated for maximum damage. Soldiers in full plate armour began to back away from the barrage.

Samuel smiled at Grug. "That man will be a blade master in a year, if I have my way. Let's go."

The two formed the back corners of a wedge of thieves that cut its way through the eastern courtyard and into the centre, where the majority of warriors were orcish or dwarven.

"Barbarian!" Giselle called, kicking an Adanan soldier off of the end of her sword. "Where have you been? You're missing all the fun!" Druskar, positioned behind her to defend her back, shook his head ruefully.

"We need to get into the keep, Giselle. We're running out of time!" Grug yelled. "Have you seen any of the gnomes?"

Bhalon and Svellin trotted up, both covered in shallow cuts, but otherwise apparently unharmed. "I saw tha gnarrinshan' a few minutes ago. 'E said tha gate ta the inner keep is blocked, an' there's troops everywhere. I do no' know if we can ge' through."

"Damn it!" Grug spat. "We're running out of time. I can feel it."

"OUT OF THE WAY," a voice boomed. Haeronor, flanked by a dozen other elvish initiates stormed into the courtyard. A golden light so deep it seemed a wall of honey flowed from every pore on the mages' bodies.

"Haeronor, they've blocked the gate. We can't get through," Grug called.

"You think not? Witness the power of the Tree and Leaf, barbarian!"

A ball of blue fire appeared before the mage, growing bigger with every second, as the elves' chanting increased in volume and speed. The orcs, dwarves and humans threw themselves to the ground as a fireball the size of the castle gates themselves seared through the air above them, crashing into the gates with a boom that knocked soldiers down across all three courtyards. A smoking crater was all that was left of the entrance to the inner keep.

Haeronor staggered to his knees, but looked up defiantly as Grug and the rest of the party climbed to their feet. "See? *That's* why you bring mages. Now…go and…finish things up. I think I need to sit down for a minute."

Dwarves and orcs closed ranks around the mages, most of whom were tottering unsteadily on their feet. Waves of arrows began falling on the enemy soldiers, as Triwathon's archers finished taking the outer walls and were able to shoot freely down into the small clusters of enemies in the courtyards.

Grug , Samuel, and Giselle led the way inside the keep, with Bhalon, Svellin, Druskar, and Marcus bringing up the rear. The air reeked of brimstone, and the warriors had to step carefully around the scorched bodies that had been blown back from the door, making Grug feel vaguely guilty. These soldiers had only been following orders, believing that their king was doing what was best for their countries. Now here they laid. Grug's jaw clenched. No. This was not his doing. These deaths were on the sorcerer's hands.

"Dungeon?" Grug asked.

Bhalon nodded. "Almos' certainly. I'tis the hardest place ta get ta, an' the mos' secure."

They started down the central stairs, weapons at the ready, but it seemed as though most of the remaining troops had been taken out by Haeronor's fire blast. Their boots and greaves clattered ominously as the party made their way down the stairs, and over to the dungeon door.

Even before he opened the door, Grug could feel the pull of the sorcerer's magic. Once it was open, it was as though a hook had gone through his navel and around his backbone, pulling him inexorably toward where the sorcerer was standing, in the middle of the design.

"Ah, my stupid barbarian friend," the sorcerer drawled, waving his hand and stopping Grug in mid-stride, though Grug could still feel the hook pulling at his guts. "And the fools that came with him. Welcome, all of you. But you're too late." He gestured at the swirling purple vortex in front of him, that was the size of a watermelon and growing slowly, but obviously, larger. "The spell is complete. The portal is opening. Nothing of this world can save you now."

Bhalon smiled grimly. "Then we shall have ta bring in a higher power, shan't we?" He raised his hammer above his head, where it began to glow with silvery light.

The sorcerer smirked. "You are out of your depth, paladin." He waved his hand, and Bhalon flew back into the dungeon wall with force enough chip the stones.

Bhalon climbed slowly to his feet. "Ye'll ha' ta do better than tha', ye mangy scum," the dwarf spat.

"With pleasure," said a firm voice from within the cell to Bhalon's right. Lanner stepped out, plunging his sword deep into Bhalon's chest. He smiled into the paladin's face.

Bhalon gurgled painfully and dropped to his knees.

"NO!" Svellin screamed, charging toward the one-eyed soldier.

The mage waved his hand again, and Svellin was thrown back through the door. With four more dismissive flicks of his wrist, he sent Giselle, Druskar, Samuel, and Marcus through the door, as well, slamming it shut behind them.

Darathan grinned malevolently as Grug's friends began to slam and pound on the door. "You, my barbarian friend, shall watch. As you were here at the beginning, so too will you be here at the end." He turned back to the portal, which was now the size of Grug's chest. "With your amulet, even the gods will not challenge me. And once they are conquered…"

Grug fought with every fibre of his being against the sorcerer's hold, reaching his boot out, ever closer, to the swirling designs on the dungeon floor. At last, with a dull scraping sound, he succeeded in dragging his toe across the stone.

The sorcerer turned. "You're stronger than I expected, I'll give you that. But it won't work, fool. The spell is etched into the stone. No one can disturb it now."

Grug's closed his eyes and concentrated, trying to come up with a solution, but all he could think of was how he needed a solution—not what that solution could be. He wished he had the other amulet; then he would know exactly what to do, but the answer seemed to lie just beyond his reach.

When Grug opened his eyes, the sorcerer's face was only inches away from his own, and the grin on it was a predatory one. "Nothing?" He laughed. "Poor barbarian. Even with that little bauble around your neck, you don't stand a chance. There is nothing that can stop me now."

There was a small cough to Grug's left. "Is it that the gnomes have been forgotten about?" Shalevelkin asked.

The sorcerer stared dumbly at the six gnomes that had just walked out of the stone wall with growing shock and horror.

The gnarrinshang gestured at the floor, and a full quarter of the sorcerer's spell disappeared, sucked into the stone. "Was it that the spell had need of all of that?"

The sorcerer's face turned the colour of spoiled milk, as the hem of his robe began to smoke. The design still beneath his feet seemed to reach, grabbing hold of him and pulling him into the rock as he screamed and smouldered. Within moments, the sorcerer had vanished, leaving only the smell of burned fur to mark his passage.

The door burst open, and Svellin charged in ahead of his companions. Lanner had already dropped his sword in surrender, leaving him nothing to stop the stocky dwarf's mace as it crashed into his chest, throwing him back into the cell he'd walked out of. Svellin dropped his weapon and knelt beside his son.

"Bhalon. Bhalon, can you hear me, son?" Tears poured down the older dwarf's cheeks as he cradled his son's head. "Speak to me."

But Bhalon's blue eyes were empty.

Svellin's wails of despair cut deeply into Grug's heart, as he watched the dwarf pull his son into his lap and rock him, his deeply graven face awash with misery and his scarred hands tracing down Bhalon's cheeks.

Grug felt anger burning within him like he had never felt before. He stalked toward the portal, which had stopped growing at a size just large enough for him to walk through, if he crouched.

"Grug!" Giselle called. "What are you doing? You can't go through there!"

Grug paused for a moment, looking at Bhalon's body and then back at Giselle. "I have a few things to say to the gods right now." He stepped into the portal, and vanished.

CHAPTER 13

BEHIND THE CURTAIN

Grug floated in nothingness. He was nothingness. Voices spun around him: "that's bullshit, Russell! You can't just kill a character off like that!"

"If a character's life points go below zero, they die. Simple."

"But I've been playing Bhalon for months! You can't just surprise attack him and kill him off. That's crap!"

Anger burned in Grug's belly, and Grug had a belly again. It seared through his veins, and his limbs reappeared. He opened his eyes.

In front of him, as though through a silken veil, lay a room. A dingy green rug lay over the floor, and strangely connected chairs covered in pillows sat before a shiny glass box. Three teenage boys and a younger girl sat on the floor with parchment on the ground in front of them, while two older boys stood over them, shouting. One of the younger boys was holding a clear drinking flask full of some bizarre green liquid, while another was eating some kind of ration that stained his mouth and fingers orange.

The second boy stared at Grug, dropping one of the orange sticks into his lap. "Uh, guys?"

One of the older boys broke off from arguing. "Not now, Josh. Damn it, Russell, you always pull something like this when you DM. You—"

"*Guys,*" the younger boy repeated.

"What?"

"Look at the shadow on the wall."

They all turned to look at Grug.

"What the hell? That looks kinda like—"

"Enough squabbling," Grug boomed.

The strange green drink crashed to the floor, as all of the players scrambled back toward a set of stairs leading up to another level.

"We will not be played with any longer," Grug said, with iron in his tone. "You took a friend from me this night, a brother. You will take nothing else." "He stepped forward, pushing on the veil, but it was unyielding. The gods scrambled back, staring at him.

"You will leave us in peace, or I will come back for you." With that, Grug turned his back on the gods, and returned to the ether.

Silence reigned in the basement for long seconds. "What. The. Hell. Was. That?" Russell asked.

Josh blinked at where the shadow of a barbarian had recently been on his wall. "I don't know, man. I think maybe we've been playing too long, though. Maybe…I dunno…Maybe too much slurpy, too. Why don't we go play some pool or something?"

"Yeah," the other older boy nodded. "Yeah…I think that's a good idea."

∗   ∗   ∗

Grug slid out of the portal and onto the floor of the dungeon, exhausted and sick. He felt himself lifted into the air like a child. "What's going on? Where are we going?"

Giselle squeezed him gently in her arms. "Home, barbarian. We're going home."

CHAPTER 14

EPILOGUE

Grug woke with a start. The fire had burned down to embers. Their glow dimly lit the room, but did little to take the chill out of the air. He squeezed his eyes shut for a moment and slowed his breathing. It had been the dream again—the void, the emptiness, and the dissolution of his body and spirit into the aether. He rarely dreamt of anything else, and wasn't sure that he would ever be rid of that feeling—being nothing, and everything all at once.

Grug shivered gently and slid from beneath the covers to grab a few sticks and place them on the fire. He crouched, blowing gently to stir the flames, and feeling the warmth grow on his face as the branches caught.

A soft snort came from the other side of the bed, and a deep, green arm crossed to his side, feeling the emptiness. Giselle's face appeared over the covers a moment later, her eyes instantly alert. "Grug?"

Grug turned back from the hearth, his vision dim from staring at the fire. "I'm here."

Giselle relaxed on hearing his voice. "Dreaming again, barbarian?"

Grug nodded.

Giselle smiled sadly at him. "It will get better."

"I know."

"Unless you start dreaming about other women. Then it will get worse. Much worse."

They laughed together.

"I don't think I could hope to handle more than one of you."

She grinned. "No, barbarian. You couldn't. But you've got one right here, who is now very much awake. Let me fill those dreams instead."

Grug smiled, and came back to bed.

If you enjoyed *Battling for the Heavens* and want to keep up with what's next for Grug Smash and his party, join my mailing list at www.nerdincognito.com/Grug-Smash. You'll get the inside scoop on new books before they come out, and free access to more content!

Reviews are an important part of the business for self-published authors. We depend on reviews to drive our books' ranking and increase sales. More sales means more content, so please take the time to review the Grug Smash novels on Amazon.

About the Author

Sean McKenzie is a father of two young boys, a devoted husband, an English M.A. degree holder, and an unabashed nerd. Bitten by the literary bug at a very early age, Sean has written dozens of short stories, plays, and, now, novels, but the Grug Smash series is the first to proceed to publication.

Sean also produces content for his website, www.nerdincognito.com, where he writes blog posts and articles about writing, literature, politics, fatherhood, DIY projects, and other nerdy pursuits.

www.ingramcontent.com/pod-product-compliance
Lightning Source LLC
Chambersburg PA
CBHW031303060726
47590CB00003B/1045